The Spell of the White Sturgeon

Jim Kjelgaard

Alpha Editions

This edition published in 2024

ISBN : 9789361471216

Design and Setting By
Alpha Editions
www.alphaedis.com
Email - info@alphaedis.com

Contents

CHAPTER ONE ....- 1 -

   STORM...- 1 -

CHAPTER TWO ....- 11 -

   WRECK ....- 11 -

CHAPTER THREE ....- 23 -

   ON THE BEACH ....- 23 -

CHAPTER FOUR...- 36 -

   TROUBLE FOR THE SPRAY.....................- 36 -

CHAPTER FIVE ....- 49 -

   RESCUE ....- 49 -

CHAPTER SIX...- 59 -

   NEW VENTURE...- 59 -

CHAPTER SEVEN ....- 72 -

   PARTNERS ....- 72 -

CHAPTER EIGHT ....- 82 -

   ACTION ....- 82 -

CHAPTER NINE...- 95 -

    PIRATES ....- 95 -

CHAPTER TEN..- 106 -

    THE GREAT FISH...- 106 -

CHAPTER ELEVEN...- 113 -

    FISHERMAN'S LUCK..- 113 -

CHAPTER TWELVE..- 122 -

    THE POND ....- 122 -

CHAPTER ONE

STORM

Ramsay Cartou leaned on the rail of the ponderous side-wheeler, the *H. H. Holter,* and watched without interest while a horse-drawn truck brought another load of cattle hides on board. The sweating stevedores who were loading the *Holter* and the belaboring mate who supervised them began stowing the hides into the hold. The *Holter's* winch, either ruined by an inexpert operator or about to fall apart anyhow, was broken. All the work had to be done by hand.

Ramsay turned to breathe the clean air that swept in from Lake Michigan. It was impossible, anywhere on the *Holter,* to get away from the smell of the hides, but at least he did not have to look at them.

Not since he had left the brawling young city of Chicago two days before, to make his way north to the equally lusty young city of Milwaukee, had the sun shone. In those two days, while he waited for repairs to the engine hauling the train in which he was riding, he had seen nothing of the lake. Now, from the mouth of the river where the *Holter* was anchored, he had a clear view, and it was exciting.

The grays of the sky and the grays of the lake were indefinable, with no clear separation. Ramsay shivered slightly.

The lake was a cat, he thought, a great sinewy cat, and the whitecaps rolling into the harbor were its sheathed and unsheathed claws. It was an awesome thing, but at the same time a wonderful one. A trembling excitement rose within him. The lake was at once a challenge and a promise—a threat and a mighty lure. He stared, fascinated, and tried to trace the rolling course of the waves as they surged toward the bank. It was impossible to follow just one for, as soon as it swelled, it retreated, to lose itself in the immense lake and renew itself in endless forward surges. Like recklessly charging soldiers, the waves cast themselves up on the bank and, exhausted, fell back.

So absorbed was he in the spectacle and so fascinated by the lake, that for a moment he was unaware of the man beside him or of the words he spoke. Then a rough hand grasped his shoulder and, reacting instantly, Ramsay whirled around.

"Why ain't you at work with the rest, boy?"

"Take your hand off me!"

The man who stood beside him was oddly like a rock, a great granite boulder. Two inches taller than Ramsay's six feet, he had a barrel chest and long, powerful arms. A leather jacket, with the sleeves cut off, hung loosely on his upper body, and beneath it he wore a homespun shirt. His black trousers had been fashioned by an exacting tailor but sadly misused. They were torn and patched with anything that might have been at hand. Black hair straggled from beneath his crushed black hat and the hair needed cutting. His eyes, colorless, were oddly inanimate, like two glass balls with no special warmth or feeling. A black beard sprouted from his cheeks and half-hid his face, but the beard did not hide thick, coarse lips. He repeated, "Them hides got to be loaded! Get to work!"

"Load them yourself!"

"I'll give you a lesson you won't forget, boy!"

"Do that!" Ramsay tensed, awaiting the anticipated attack of the bigger, heavier man. He felt almost a grim pleasure. He had learned his fighting the hard way, as anybody brought up on the New York water-front, and with an irresponsible father had to learn it. The man who faced him was heavier by a good sixty pounds, but he was a bull of a man and, probably, he would fight like a bull. Would he know about matadors?

The man's eyes were narrowed to pinpoints, and they seemed to spark. Sheer rage made his face livid, while his lips were distorted in a snarl. He drew back, readying himself for the spring that would overwhelm this brash youth who had dared dispute him. Ramsay poised on lithe feet, prepared to side-step.

Then fat, fussy little Captain Schultz, skipper of the *Holter*, stepped between them. He wheezed like an over-fat lap-dog, "Vot you doin'?"

"I want them hides loaded and the ship under way!" the man who faced Ramsay snarled.

"Ach! Dis man payin' passenger!"

A deck hand, his eyes downcast, hurried past. The man who had ordered Ramsay to get to work stood still for a moment, glaring. Then, furiously, soundlessly, he turned on his heel and strode up the gangplank to the pier. Ramsay watched him go, and he knew that, even if there had not been unpleasantness between them, he could never like this man. No matter where they met, or how, they would never get along together.

Captain Schultz also turned to watch the man depart. Then he gave his attention to Ramsay.

"Ach! You should be careful 'pout startin' fights, poy."

"So should other people!" Ramsay said, still smarting.

"You should, too. Yaah!"

And, as though he had settled that once and for all, Captain Schultz waddled away to speak to the mate who was supervising the stevedores. A little uncertainty arose in Ramsay.

This—this half-wilderness, half-civilization in which he found himself was a land of strong contradictions. Lake Michigan, with all its fear and all its terror, and all its inspiration, lapped the Wisconsin shores. Yet some man could be so little impressed by the vast lake that he could name a boat for himself. Possibly a man capable of building or owning a ship like the *Holter* had a right to think of himself.

Ramsay turned again to look at the lake, and his mind projected him far away from the worn, slippery decks of the *Holter.* Almost he was unaware of the two silver dollars in his pocket, all the money he had left in the world, and of the uncertain future. At the same time, while his inmost being feasted on the lake, a part of his mind reviewed the events that had brought him here. He had an abrupt, uncomfortable revival of a New York memory.

There was a lion, a great, black-maned lion, in the New York zoo. It was well fed and well cared for, its every need attended. But most times the lion had still seemed restless and unhappy, and sometimes it had been a tired thing. Then it was hardly a lion at all but just a weary, living thing. Ramsay had wondered often how that lion felt.

He had never decided exactly how it did feel; within himself there were a dozen conflicting opinions. The lion paced its cage, and coming to the end of the very narrow limits granted to it, it turned and went back the other way. Coming to the end of the cage, it turned again. But all it ever found was the place it had already left. Once in a great while the lion had been very alert and very attentive. It was as though, now and again, the great animal could scent a wind of which nothing else was aware. That wind brought him memories of freedom, and happiness and the unhampered jungle life that had been.

Ramsay had gone often to see the lion, and though he never understood why, he always felt as though he had something in common with it, and he understood it partially. New York offered an abundance of opportunities, but they were well bound and well defined. There had always been a wild longing, a reckless yearning, within him, and often he thought that the newspapers which carried stories of the undeveloped Midwest were to him what the faint jungle scents had been to the lion. He had devoured every story eagerly. The Midwest was new, the papers had said. Good farm land, if one wanted to be a farmer, could be had for as little as four dollars an acre. It was the land of the future.

Again Ramsay jingled the two dollars in his pocket. He had answered the call of the Midwest because he could not help answering it. He had to try and to go and see for himself, but at the same time a caution, inborn in his Scotch mother and transplanted to him, could not be ignored. Before he burned his bridges behind him he had wanted to make sure that there were some ahead, and correspondence with the manager of the Three Points tannery had led to the offer of a job when he came. A dollar and twenty-five cents a day the tannery was offering able-bodied men, and there were too few men.

Ramsay looked out upon the lake, and a little thrill of excitement swept through him. Sometimes he had felt doubts about the wisdom of having left New York for the Midwest. He had been sure of a place to sleep and enough to eat as long as he stayed in New York, and again he felt the two dollars in his pocket.

Troubled, he looked out on the surging lake, and knew an instant peace. It was worth seeing. It was something few New Yorkers ever saw. The ocean was at their doorstep, and few of them even bothered looking at that; but the ocean was not like this. Lake Michigan was fresh and clean, different, wild and, as the papers had promised, new. Ramsay tasted the wet air, liking it as he did so.

He turned at a sudden squealing and clatter on the pier, and saw four men trying to fight a little black horse onto the ship. The horse, not trusting this strange craft and certainly not liking it, lashed out with striking hooves. Dodging, the men finally fought it into a sort of small cage they had prepared. The horse thrust its head over the side and bugled shrilly.

Ramsay watched interestedly, distracted for the few minutes the men needed to get the horse into its cage. It reared as though it would climb over the confining bars, then stood quietly. A sensible horse, Ramsay decided, and a good one. Only fools, whether they were animals or men, fought when there was no chance of winning or battered their brains out against a stone wall. Good animals and good men never considered anything hopeless, but they tried to fight with intelligence as well as brawn. Ramsay glanced again at the horse.

It was standing quietly but not resignedly. Its head was up. Its ears were alert and its eyes bright. It still did not like the ship, but it had not just given in. Rather, it was waiting a good chance to get away. Ramsay grinned. The next time, he decided, they would have a little more trouble getting that horse onto anything that floated. Then he returned his attention to the loading of the *Holter*.

A continuous line of horse-drawn trucks loaded with hides was coming alongside the ship, and the stevedores were laboring mightily to stow the hides away. Obviously whoever owned the *Holter* intended to load her with every last pound she would carry. He wanted a paying cargo that would pay off to the last cent. Almost imperceptibly the ship settled into the water. The gangplank, that had been almost even with the deck, now tilted downward.

Once or twice Ramsay saw the bearded, jacketed man with whom he had quarreled. But the man did not venture onto the *Holter* again. Rather, he seemed more interested in getting the hides loaded. Ramsay speculated on the scene he was witnessing, and then he found the whys and wherefores, the reasons behind it.

This Wisconsin country was still more than half a wilderness. It had its full share of wilderness men, but its fertile farm lands were attracting many Dutch, Swiss and German farmers. Struggling with a half-tamed country, they did anything they could to earn a livelihood, and some of them raised beef cattle. The hides were a by-product and the world markets needed leather. But the leather could not be processed without necessary materials, and the hemlock trees which provided tan bark were being cut at Three Points. It was cheaper, and easier, to transport the hides to Three Points than it was to carry the cumbersome tan bark to Milwaukee or Chicago. From Three Points, harness leather, sole leather and almost every other kind, was shipped by boat to Chicago and from there it was carried to the eastern markets by rail.

It was not until mid-afternoon that the last of the hides were loaded and the hatches battened down. The side wheel began to turn and the *Holter* moved cumbersomely down the river into Lake Michigan. Standing in his enclosure, the little horse stamped restlessly and neighed again. He was nervous, but he was not afraid.

Ramsay approved. The little black horse didn't like his cage, but he would meet the situation as it existed rather than lose his head or become panic-stricken. Ramsay walked over to the cage and the horse thrust his velvet muzzle against the bars. When the boy rubbed his nose, the horse twitched his ears and looked at him with friendly eyes.

Thick smoke belched from the *Holter's* stack and made a long plume over the lake, behind the plodding side-wheeler. A strong wind was screaming in from the north and lashing the water angrily into leaping waves. The ship nosed into the trough created by the waves and rose again on the opposite side. Ramsay walked to the bow and leaned over the rail, and a mighty excitement rose anew within him.

This, it seemed, was what he had wanted to find when he left New York to go roving. The lake, storm-lashed, was a wild and terrible thing. It was a beast, but something with a vast appeal lay behind its fury and its anger. Lake Michigan was the place for a man. It would never be free of challenge if there was anyone who dared to pick up the gauntlet it cast.

There was motion beside Ramsay, and the deck hand who had passed while he argued with the bearded man fell in beside him. He glanced at the man. The deck hand was about thirty-six, older than Ramsay by eighteen years, and there was a seasoned, weather-beaten look about him. It was as though he had turned his face to many a raging storm and many a fierce wind.

He grinned amiably. "Hi!"

"Hi!" Ramsay said.

The deck hand chuckled. "Boy, I thought you were in trouble sure when you were ruckusin' with old Devil Chad."

"Devil Chad?"

"Yeah. The one who told you to help load hides. He'd of cleaned the deck with you."

"Maybe he would," Ramsay said. "And then again, maybe he wouldn't."

"He would," the deck hand asserted. "He can lick anybody or anything. Owns half the country 'round here, he does, includin' most of the *Holter*. What's more, he aims to keep it. One of the richest men in Wisconsin."

"Quite a man," Ramsay said drily.

"Yeah, an' quite a fighter. On'y reason he didn't clean your clock was on account Captain Schultz told him you was a payin' passenger. Devil Chad, he gets half the fare every passenger on the *Holter* pays, he does."

Ramsay knew a rising irritation. "What makes you so sure he can't be cut down to size?"

"Never has been, never will be," the deck hand asserted. He regarded the surging lake morosely, and then said, "One of these days this old tub is goin' to end up right at the bottom of Michigan, it is. Either that or on the beach. Wish I was some'res else."

"Why don't you go somewhere else?"

"One of these days I will," the deck hand threatened. "I'll just haul off an' go back to the ocean boats, I will. I was on 'em for fourteen years, an' quit to come here on account I got scar't of storms at sea. Ha! Worstest thing I ever see on the Atlantic ain't nothin' to what this lake can throw at you."

"Is it really that bad?" Ramsay asked eagerly.

"Bad?" the deck hand said. "Boy, I've seen waves here taller'n a ship. In course nobody ever goes out when it's that bad on account, if they did, nobody'd ever get back." He scanned the horizon. "We're goin' to hit weather afore we ever gets to Three Points. Goin' to hit it sure. Wish this old tub wasn't loaded so heavy, an' with hides at that."

A wave struck the bow, crested and broke in foaming spray that cast itself up and over the ship. Ramsay felt it, cool on his face, and he licked eager lips. Lake Michigan was fresh water, not salt like the ocean, and it was as pure as an ice-cold artesian well. It was also, he thought, almost as cold.

He looked into the clouded horizon, studying the storm that battered the *Holter*. He smiled to himself.

Suddenly he became all eager interest, peering out into the driving waves and focusing his attention on one place. He thought he had seen something there, but because of the angry lake he could not be sure. It might have been just a drifting shadow, or just one more of the dark waves which seemed to fill the lake and to be of all shades. Then, and plainly, he saw it again.

It was a boat, a little boat no more than twenty-four feet from bowsprit to stern, and it was carrying almost a full load of sail as it tacked back and forth into the wind. Ramsay had not seen the sails because, when he first spotted the boat, it had been heeled over so far that the sails did not show. Now they were showing and full, and the little boat sailed like a proud swan with its wings spread.

Ramsay forgot the *Holter*, the man beside him and everything else save the little boat. The *Holter* and nothing on it, with the possible exception of the little black horse, was even remotely interesting. But this was. Ramsay breathed a sigh of relief.

He should have known. He should have understood from the first that, when any water was as mighty and as exciting as Lake Michigan, there would be some to meet its challenge with daring, grace and spirit. The tiny craft was a mere cockleshell of a boat, a ridiculously small thing with which to venture upon such a water, but Ramsay could not help feeling that it would be much better to sail on the little boat than on the *Holter*.

He kept fascinated eyes on it as it tacked back into the wind. Again it heeled over, so far that it was almost hidden in the trough of a vast wave. Saucily, jauntily it bobbed up again.

The *Holter*, that workhorse of the water, plodded stolidly on its appointed way. Ramsay continued to watch the little boat, and now they were near enough so that he could see its crew of four. He gasped involuntarily.

Working into the wind, the little boat was coming back, and its course took it directly across the *Holter's* right of way. Ramsay clenched his fingers and bit his lip fiercely. A collision seemed inevitable. Wide-eyed, he watched the little boat.

Now he saw its name, not painted on with stencils but written in a fine, free-flowing script, *Spray*, and the carved Valkyrie maiden that was its figurehead. A big gull, obviously its tame one, sat on the very top of the mast and flapped its wings. The *Spray* had a crew of four, but Ramsay concentrated on just one of them.

He was huge, fully as tall as the black beard who had accosted Ramsay and just as heavy, but he was a different kind of man. He balanced on his little boat's swaying deck with all the grace of a dancer, while he clung almost carelessly to a line that ran through a pulley.

No inch of the man's shirt and trousers, which were all the clothing he wore, for he was bare-footed, remained dry, and the shaggy blond curls that carpeted his head were dripping. White teeth gleamed as he looked up at the *Holter* and laughed. Ramsay leaned forward excitedly. He warmed to this man, even as he had been repelled by the black beard the deck hand called Devil Chad. The man on the boat was gay and spirited, and he seemed complete master of everything about him.

The deck hand put cupped hands to his mouth and screamed, "Sheer off! Sheer off!"

Captain Schultz's voice was heard. "*Dumkopf!* Go 'way!"

Then, just as it seemed that collision could not be avoided, more sail bloomed on the *Spray's* mast and she danced lightly out of the way. The man with the shaggy curls looked back and waved a taunting hand. Ramsay turned to watch, but the *Spray* disappeared in a curtain of mist that had draped itself between the *Holter* and the shore. His eyes shining, the boy turned to the deck hand.

"Who was that?"

"A crazy Dutch fisherman, named Hans Van Doorst," the deck hand growled. "He'd sail that peanut shell right in to see Old Nick hisself, an' one of these days he will. He ain't even afraid of the White Sturgeon."

"What's the White Sturgeon?"

The deck hand looked at him queerly. "How long you been here, boy?"

"A couple of days."

"Well, that accounts for it. You see the White Sturgeon; you start prayin' right after. You'll need to. Nobody except that crazy Van Doorst has ever saw him an' lived to tell about it. Well, got to get to work."

The deck hand wandered away. Ramsay turned again to face the storm and let spray blow into his face. He thought of all that had happened since he had, at last, reached Lake Michigan. This Wisconsin country was indeed a land of sharp contrasts.

The *Holter* and the *Spray*. Captain Schultz and the deck hand. Devil Chad and Hans Van Doorst. A tannery and a fisherman. Local superstition about a white sturgeon. Ramsay knew a rising satisfaction. This semi-wilderness, lapped by a vast inland sea, might be a strange land, but nobody could say that it was not an interesting or a strong one. His last lingering doubts were set at rest and for the first time he was entirely satisfied because he had come. A strong country was always the place for strong people.

Ramsay raised his head, puzzled by something which, suddenly, seemed to be out of place. For a second he did not know what it was. Then he realized that the crying gulls which had been following the *Holter* in the hope that scraps or garbage would be tossed to them or else interested in whatever debris the side wheel might churn up, were no longer there.

Ramsay knew a second's uneasiness, and he could not explain it. He did not know why he missed the gulls. It was just that they and their crying had seemed a part of the lake. Now that they were gone, the lake was incomplete. The boy braced himself against a sudden, vicious burst of wind.

Even a land-lubber could tell that the storm's fury was increasing. A sharp patter of rain sliced like a shower of cold knives across the *Holter's* deck, and Ramsay ducked his head. He raised it again, grinning sheepishly as he did so, then gripped the rail to steady himself. He watched with much interest as the storm raged even more strongly.

It was driving directly out of the northwest, and it seemed to be perpetually re-born in the dark clouds that had possession of the sky. A howling wind accompanied it, and more shrapnel-bursts of rain.

The waves rose to prodigious heights. Dipping into them, the *Holter* seemed no more than a leaf on this tossing sea. Turning, Ramsay saw the helmsman clinging almost fiercely to his wheel, as though he would somehow soften the storm's rage by doing that. In his cage the little black horse nickered uncertainly.

Then there came something that was instantly apparent, even above the screaming wind. The rough rhythm of the *Holter's* throbbing engines seemed to halt. The ship shivered mightily, as though in pain.

The engines stopped.

CHAPTER TWO

WRECK

Shorn of her power, the *Holter* still followed her helmsman's course. But it became a listless, sluggish course. The ship was like a suddenly freed slave that does not know what to do with his own freedom.

For six years she had plodded Lake Michigan, always with the biggest possible paying load and always working at top speed. Many times she had groaned and protested, but she had been forced to obey the dictates of the engine that turned her side wheel. Now the engine, the tyrant, was dead from misuse of its own power. But without it the *Holter* had neither mind nor will of her own.

She smashed head-on into a mountainous wave that set her decks awash. For another moment or two she held her course, carried by her own momentum. Then, slowly and unwillingly, as though afraid to do such a thing and not trusting herself to do it, she swung broadside to the waves.

A muffled shout floated out of the engine room. Fat little Captain Schultz, a slicker covering his round body and anxiety written on his face, was peering down an opened hatch. Sluicing rain pelted the slicker and bounded off. Ramsay's eyes found the deck hand.

Eyes wide and mouth agape, he was standing near the wheelhouse. Naked terror was written on his face as he stared at something out in the lake. Ramsay followed his gaze.

To the starboard, the right side of the *Holter*, the lake seemed strangely calm. It was as though the wind and the storm did not strike with outrageous strength there, and oddly as if that part of the water might be commanded by some inexplicable force. Unable to tear his gaze away, expecting to see something special, Ramsay kept his eyes riveted on the calm water.

He saw a ripple, but not one born of storm and wind. There was something here that had nothing to do with the driving wind, or the cold rain, or even the tremendous waves. The deck hand covered his eyes with his hand.

At that instant, a great white apparition swam up through the water. It was a ghost, a creature of nightmares, a terrible thing seen only in terror-ridden moments. Ramsay controlled an impulse to shout or to flee. The thing came up to within inches of the surface and wallowed there like a greasy fat hog. Whitish-gray, rather than pure white, it flipped an enormous tail while it sported near the surface.

The thing, a fish, seemed fully nine feet long and possibly it carried a hundred pounds of weight for every foot. It bore no scales but seemed to be clothed in an overlapping series of armored plates. Its snout, pointed somewhat like a pig's, was tipped with barbels, or feelers. Dull eyes showed.

Again Ramsay controlled his fear. The thing, sober judgment told him, was nothing more or less than a great sturgeon, the mightiest fish of these inland waters. The fact that it was white, rather than the conventional gray-green or olive-green, was of no significance whatever. All living creatures, from elephants down to mice, occasionally produced an albino. It was not beyond reason that there could be an albino sturgeon.

Ramsay watched while it swam, and some semblance of cool control returned to his fevered imagination. This was no grotesque monster from another world. Telling himself again that it was nothing more or less than an unusual fish, he watched it sink back into the churning depths from which it had arisen. He put a shaking hand on the *Holter's* rail.

It was a fish and nothing else. None but superstitious people believed in superstition. Then the deck hand's terrified shriek rose above the keening wind.

"It's him! We seen it! The White Sturgeon! *Gar-hhh!*"

Mouth agape, the deck hand kept his eyes on that place where the White Sturgeon had disappeared. A great wave washed across the deck, and when it rolled away the deck hand was no longer visible. Ramsay shook his head to clear it and looked again at the place where the deck hand had been standing. Lake Michigan could swallow a man even easier than a pond swallowed a pebble, for there had not been even a ripple to mark the place where the deck hand had disappeared. There was not the slightest possibility of rescuing him. The deck hand had seen the White Sturgeon!

A battering ram of a wave crashed into the *Holter's* starboard side, and Ramsay felt a cold chill travel up and down his spine. Fear laid its icy fingers there, but he shook them off. The fact that the water had been calm when the White Sturgeon made its appearance and was angry now had nothing whatever to do with the fish. Rather, the calm water could be attributed to some quirk, some phenomenon inherent in the storm itself. Probably the White Sturgeon appeared because, for the moment, the lake had been calm. Knowing that, the big fish had nosed its way to the surface. Now that the lake was again storm-deviled, the White Sturgeon was gone.

Bracing himself against the wind, Ramsay made his way across the deck to the wheelhouse. He shivered, for the first time aware of the fact that his clothing was rain-drenched and that he was very cold. It was a penetrating, creeping cold that reached the inmost marrow of his bones. When another wave smashed the *Holter*, Ramsay caught hold of the little horse's cage to steady himself. Within the enclosure, nervous but still not terrified, the black horse looked hopefully at him.

Ramsay reached the wheelhouse, and came face to face with Captain Schultz. The little captain's slicker had blown open, so that now it was of no use whatever in warding off the rain, but he had not seen fit to close it again. It would do him no good if he did; his clothing was already soaked.

Ramsay shouted to make himself heard above the roar of the wind. "What happened?"

"The enchin, she kaput. Like that, she kaput."

Ramsay revised his opinions of the little Captain. At the pier, Captain Schultz had been only a fat, fussy little man. Facing this dire predicament, he was not terrified and had not given way to panic. He had risen to the emergency. Maybe, Ramsay thought, anyone who sailed Lake Michigan had to be able to rise to any emergency if he would continue to sail. He shouted again, "Will the ship sink?"

"Ach, I don't know! If we can't get the enchin to go, she might."

"What do we do then?"

"Find somet'ing. Find anyt'ing, poy, an' swim. Be sure you find somet'ing that does not sink mit you."

"How far are we from land?"

"Ach! That I cannot tell you."

"Did you see the White Sturgeon?"

"Yaah. We still try."

Captain Schultz went all the way into the wheelhouse and disappeared into the hold. Dimly, out of the open hatchway, came the sound of ringing hammers. There was a desperate tone in them, as though the men working in the *Holter's* hold were fully aware of the grave danger they faced. On sudden impulse Ramsay ducked into the wheelhouse and descended into the engine-room.

Captain Schultz held an oil lamp to illumine the labors of two men whom, so far, Ramsay had not seen. Presumably they were the *Holter's* engineer and fireman. Another deck hand and the mate stood by, passing tools requested by the workers.

Down here, in the bowels of the *Holter*, the storm seemed a faraway and almost an unreal thing. The howling wind was heard faintly, and if the ship had not been tossing so violently, they might have been in the power-room of any industrial plant.

The sweating engineer, his face grease-streaked, turned from his labors to face Ramsay. He spoke with a nasal New England twang. "Was that White Sturgeon really off the ship?"

"I—I didn't see anything," Ramsay answered.

Captain Schultz flashed him a grateful smile. The workers went on with their toils.

Obviously, among Lake Michigan sailors, or anyhow some of them, there was a firm belief in the evil powers of the White Sturgeon. Ramsay looked again at the little Captain's face.

It was a concerned, worried face, what one might expect to see in a man who was in danger of losing his ship. At the same time, and even though Captain Schultz remained completely in command, there was about him a certain air that had nothing to do with getting the *Holter's* engine working again. Ramsay sought for the answer, and finally he found it. A strong man in his own right, Captain Schultz had seen the White Sturgeon and he believed in it.

Ramsay climbed the narrow ladder-way leading back to the deck. The *Holter* was strong, he assured himself. There was little danger that it could be pounded to pieces by any sea. Then he looked at the wild and angry lake and knew the fallacy of his reasoning.

The *Holter* was strong, but the lake was stronger. Waves, the color of steel and with the strength of steel, smashed into the ship and made her shiver. Ramsay heard a shrieking protest as some plank or stay beneath the deck tore loose.

The *Holter* shuddered, like a big horse in pain, and settled so low in the water that waves washed continuously across her deck. There was another shriek, and she settled deeper into the lake. She was a very sluggish craft now, with no control or direction, and Ramsay guessed that the hides in the hold were getting soaked. The ship's nose dipped to meet a wave, and it did not come up again.

The imprisoned horse bugled his fright. Captain Schultz, the engineer, the fireman and the deck hand appeared on deck. There was no sign of the mate; perhaps he had already gone over. The engineer and the fireman struggled under the weight of a crude raft which they had knocked together from such timbers as were available. Ramsay looked uncertainly toward them, and the engineer glared back.

"Get your own!" he snarled. "Me an' Pete made this, an' me an' Pete are goin' to use it!"

They carried their makeshift raft to the settling nose of the ship, laid it down, mounted it, and let the next wave carry them off. Ramsay felt a turning nausea in the pit of his stomach. As the raft went over the rail, the man called Pete was swept from it. Only the engineer stayed on, clinging desperately as he was washed out into the angry lake. In a second or two he had disappeared.

Captain Schultz rolled frightened eyes and said to Ramsay, "Get a door, or hatch cover, an' ride that."

Suiting his actions to his words, Captain Schultz seized a fire axe that was hanging near and pounded the wheelhouse door from its hinges. He dragged the door to the rail, threw it into the lake, and jumped after it. The deck hand wrestled with a hatch cover, finally pried it loose, and rode that away.

Ramsay was left alone on the sinking *Holter*. He tried to keep a clear head, but he could not help an overwhelming fear. This was nothing he had ever faced before and now, facing it, he did not know what to do. Finding anything that would float and riding it away seemed to be the answer. Then the little horse bugled and he knew that he was not alone.

Water crept around his feet as he made his way across the deck to the cage. He put his hand on the bar, and as soon as he did that the little horse thrust a soft, warm nose against it. He muzzled Ramsay's hand with almost violent intensity. All his life he had depended upon men for everything. Now, in this peril, men would not desert him.

Softly Ramsay stroked the soft muzzle, but only for a second. The *Holter* was going down fast. Soon, as the gloomy deck hand had forecast, she would be on the bottom of Lake Michigan. There was no time to lose. Ramsay unlatched the door of the cage, opened it, and when he did that the horse walked out.

He stayed very near to the boy, fearing to leave, and once or twice bumped Ramsay with his shoulder. Ramsay studied the angry lake, and looked back at the horse. Again he glanced out on the stormy water. There was nothing else in sight. Those who, by one way or another, hoped to reach shore were already lost in swirling sheets of rain. Ramsay bit his lower lip so hard that he drew blood.

The men had either jumped, or else had merely ridden over the rail on a wave that set the decks awash, but the horse could not do that. There was real danger of his breaking a leg, or becoming otherwise injured, if he tried. Ramsay turned and caught up the axe with which Captain Schultz had stricken down the door.

The black horse crowded with him, afraid to be alone, and the boy had to go around him to get back to the rail. The horse pushed close to him again and Ramsay spoke soothingly, "Easy. Take it easy now."

He raised the axe and swung it, and felt its blade bite deeply into the wooden rail. He swung again and again, until he had slashed through it, then moved ten feet to one side, toward the rail's supporting post, and cut it there. The severed section was whisked into the wave-tormented lake as a match stick disappears in a whirlpool. Ramsay threw the axe back onto the *Holter's* sinking deck and stepped aside.

Get something that would float, Captain Schultz had said, and be sure that it would keep him above water. But suddenly he could think of nothing that would float. Wildly he cast about for a hatch cover or a door. There was not one to be seen.

The *Holter* made a sudden list that carried her starboard deck beneath the lake. A wave surged across her. Even the little horse had unsteady legs. Ramsay tried hard to overcome the terror within him.

Then, together, he and the little horse were in the lake. He threw wild arms about the animal's neck, and a huge wave overwhelmed them. Gasping, he arose.

The lake was wilder and fiercer and colder than he had thought it could be. Every nerve and muscle in his body seemed chilled, so that he was barely able to move. Another wave washed in, over both the little black horse and himself, and for a moment they were deep beneath the churning waters. They broke onto the surface, Ramsay with both hands entwined in the horse's mane, and the horse turned to look at him.

There was uncertainty in the animal's eyes, and fright, but no terror. The little horse knew his own power, and the fact that a human being stayed with him gave him confidence in that strength.

Ramsay spoke reassuringly. "We're all right. We'll do all right, Black. Let's get out of it."

The words were a tonic, the inspiration the horse needed. The next time a wave rolled in, he did not try to fight it. Rather, he rose with it, swimming strongly. He had adjusted himself to many situations, now he met this one without panic. An intelligent beast, he had long ago learned that every crisis must be met with intelligence.

Ramsay stayed easily beside him, keeping just enough weight on the swimming animal to hold his own head above water and doing nothing that would interfere with the furious fight the horse was waging to keep from drowning.

The lake was indeed cold, colder than any other water the boy had ever known, and he had to exercise every particle of his mind and will just to cling to the horse. The wind blew furiously, and sluicing rain poured down. Then the rain dwindled away and heavy mist settled in. Ramsay knew a moment's panic.

It was impossible to see more than a few feet or to tell which way the shore lay. The lake was huge, and should they be heading towards the Michigan shore, they would never get there. Ramsay tried to remember all he had ever known of wind and drift and currents on Lake Michigan, and discovered that he could remember nothing. Any direction at all could be north and he was unable to orient himself, but he controlled the rising panic. It would do no good at all to lose his head.

The wind seemed to be dying, and the waves lessening. Ramsay kept his hold on the little horse's mane. He saw a floating object pass and tried to catch it, but when he did so he almost lost his hold on the horse. Kicking hard to catch up, he twined both hands in the horse's mane and tightened them there.

Then he felt a rebirth of confidence. Already they had been in the lake for a long, long time and he had been able to hold his own. It was impossible to get much colder, or more numb, than he already was and he could still hang on. Besides, the horse seemed to know where he was going.

He swam strongly, and apparently he was swimming straight. At any rate, there was no evidence that he was traveling in circles or choosing an erratic course. Ramsay had been told that animals have an instinct compared to which the most sensitive human's is coarse and blunted and maybe that was true. Maybe the horse did know where it was going.

Now that the waves were not rising so high, the horse swam faster. The wind died almost completely, so that the lake's surface was merely ruffled, and Ramsay felt a mounting confidence in his ability to live through this. In the overcast a gull cried, and things had started going wrong with the *Holter* when the gulls left it. Now they were back. Probably they, too, had known of the approaching storm and had flown to safety off the lake.

The swimmers broke out of the mist and Ramsay saw the beach.

It was about a hundred yards away, a sand beach behind which a rocky cliff rose. This wore a crest of evergreens, and its face was spotted here and there with smaller trees. A cloud of white gulls screamed into the air as Ramsay and the horse approached.

They reached the shallows, and the little horse's back emerged from the water like that of some suddenly appearing sea monster. Ramsay let go his hold on the animal's mane and swam. Then, coming to waist-high water in which he could wade, he splashed toward the beach.

The wind had died, but waves still pounded the beach and it was very cold. The near borders of this wild lake, Ramsay decided, probably never warmed up. With an immense body of cold water lapping them, they were perpetually chilled.

While the little horse looked gravely on, Ramsay stripped his clothing off, wrung it out, and put the wet garments back on. The horse crowded very close, as though he were afraid to go away. He nibbled Ramsay with his lips. As soon as the boy moved, he moved with him.

He stayed very near as Ramsay walked up the beach, a stretch of driftwood-spotted sand that varied from sixty to two hundred feet in width and reached clear back to the rising bluff. A belt of wet sand showed where the lake had crawled up onto the beach and fallen back.

The boy stopped suddenly, and the little horse stopped with him. Just ahead, in the belt of wet sand which the highest waves had washed, lay two tumbled figures. The little horse tossed his head uneasily, not liking this at all, and Ramsay felt a cold lump rise in his throat. He advanced at a slow walk and, after some hesitation, the horse trotted to catch up with him. Ramsay stopped again.

The two drowned people were Captain Schultz of the *Holter* and the deck hand who had wished so fervently that he was somewhere else. Ramsay cleared the lump in his throat, and was struck by the notion that at last the deck hand had gone somewhere else. Then the black horse raised his head and nickered, and the boy looked around to see a man on a spotted black-and-white horse riding toward him.

He rode at full trot, the reins hanging loosely around his mount's throat, and he wore an outlandish sort of affected cowboy's hat pulled low over his eyes. His features were heavy, and would be flabby when he had aged a few more years. Blue jeans clung tightly around his legs, and straight black hair lay thick on his head. As he rode, he leveled a heavy pistol.

"Go on! Beat it!"

"But ..."

"This is my find! I said beat it!"

The pistol roared, and a heavy ball buried itself in the sand at Ramsay's feet. The boy felt a quick anger and a disinclination to obey the order to leave. He took a step toward the horseman, knowing that he would need a few seconds to re-load his pistol. But almost by magic another pistol appeared in the man's hand and he leveled it steadily.

"Your last warnin'. Go on!"

Ramsay shrugged, and the black horse followed him as he walked on. This was indeed a strange land, where men were willing to fight for the possession of corpses. What did the horseman want with them? The loot they might have in their pockets? Perhaps, but that seemed very unlikely. Captain Schultz was not the type of person who would carry a great deal of money in his pockets, and certainly the deck hand wouldn't have enough to bother about. But obviously the horseman wanted the two bodies.

Ramsay walked on up the sand beach. Gulls rose protestingly as he came in sight, and flocks of ducks scudded across the water. A pair of Canada Geese hissed at him as he passed. They were guarding a nest and they were ready to fight for it. Ramsay gave them a wide berth and the horse walked faithfully beside him.

The afternoon was half-spent when Ramsay smelled wood smoke. He quickened his pace, but remained cautious. This was a wild land, with no part of it wilder than this lonely Lake Michigan Beach, and there was never any certainty as to just what anyone would find or how he would be received. Nevertheless, if these people were friendly, other humans would be welcome. Ramsay was both hungry and tired to the point of exhaustion. He fingered the two dollars in his pocket. He could pay his way. He rounded a long, forested nose of land where the bluff cut the sand beach to a narrow five feet and looked out on a peaceful bay.

The bluff gave way to gently rising, treeless hills. A rail fence hemmed part of them in, and black-and-white cattle grazed inside the fence. A stone house, of Dutch architecture, stood on a knoll that commanded a view of the lake, and a suitable distance from it was a snug wooden barn. A small lake, or large pond, separated from Lake Michigan by a narrow neck of land, glowed like a blue sapphire. Chickens, ducks and geese crowded noisily together in the barnyard, and a man with a wooden pail in his hand came out of the barn door.

Ramsay walked forward, as first uncertainly and then very steadily. A man might be afraid, but it was always to his advantage not to let the enemy, if enemy this might be, know he was afraid. The man at the barn door hesitated, and then stood still while the boy approached.

Ramsay greeted him pleasantly, "Hello."

"Hello."

The man was tall and supple, with a frank, open face and intelligent, blue eyes. He was perhaps six years older than Ramsay and he spoke with a Dutch accent. Ramsay said, "I was sailing up to Three Points on the *Holter*. Now she's wrecked and I must walk...."

"The *Holter's* wrecked?" the other broke in.

"Yes."

"Any drowned people on the beach?"

"Two, but a man on a black-and-white horse took them away from me at pistol point." Ramsay knew a rising impatience. "Why the dickens should he do that?"

The other grinned faintly. "You get money for watching 'em until they can be brought in and buried proper, and money is not easy to come by. If there's a man already watching these, that would be Joe Mannis. He combs the beach night and day after storms, and he's got as much money as most people. What can I do for you?"

"I'd like something to eat before I go on to Three Points."

"That we can give you," the farmer said. "Come."

When the horse would have followed them to the house, the Dutch farmer looked quizzically at Ramsay. The boy grinned.

"He's not mine. He was on the *Holter* and we swam ashore together. Without him I might not have made it."

"Then he is yours," the farmer said. "By right of salvage he is yours. But Marta, she wouldn't like a horse in the house."

"It's hardly the place for a horse," Ramsay agreed. "Can we leave him here?"

"Yaah."

The farmer opened the barnyard gate and Ramsay walked in. The horse followed willingly. Ramsay stepped out and shut the gate. He saw the little horse, its head over the bars, watching him as he walked toward the house.

It was a clean house, and a scrubbed and shiny one. Even the big flat stone that served as a back doorstep had almost an antiseptic cleanliness. The house was filled with the odors of freshly baked bread and spice and canned jam and curing hams. Ramsay smiled at the slim, pleasant girl who met them at the door.

"Marta," the farmer said, "this man was ship-wrecked and is to be our guest for as long as he wants to stay. He is...?"

"Ramsay Cartou," Ramsay supplied.

"Yaah! Ramsay Cartou. I am Pieter Van Hooven and this is my wife, Marta."

Ramsay made himself comfortable in the neat kitchen while Marta Van Hooven hurried efficiently about, preparing a meal. There was baked whitefish, venison, roasted goose, fluffy mashed potatoes, crisp salad, billowy fresh rolls, delicious cheese and milk.

Ramsay ate until he could eat no more, then pushed himself away from the table and smiled graciously at Marta Van Hooven. "That was good!" he said feelingly.

"You ate so little."

Ramsay grinned, "Not more than enough to feed three good-sized horses. You can really cook."

Pieter Van Hooven glowed at this compliment extended to his wife. He filled and lighted a clay pipe, and puffed contentedly. "What are you going to do now?" he asked Ramsay.

"I," Ramsay hesitated, "I'd like to pay for the meal."

Pieter Van Hooven smiled. "Forget that. You were our guest."

"How far is Three Points?"

"Six miles. Just stay on the beach."

"Reckon I'll go up there then. I've got a job waiting for me at the tannery. By the way, do you have any use for that horse?"

"A good horse can always be used on a farm. But I won't take him. I'll keep him, and you can have him any time you want." Pieter Van Hooven looked queerly at Ramsay. "You sure you want to go to Three Points?"

"I've got a job there, and I need it."

"Then go, but remember that nobody starves in Wisconsin. Marta and me, we got no money but we got everything else. You don't like it in Three Points, you might come back here?"

"I'll be glad to," Ramsay said, a little puzzled.

"Then do that, my friend."

Well-fed and rested, Ramsay walked alone up the sandy beach. Stay on the sand, Pieter Van Hooven had advised him, and he couldn't go wrong. Three Points, the tannery town, was right on the lake. Two hours after he left the Van Hoovens, Ramsay reached the village.

Three Points nestled snugly in a gap which, only recently, had been hacked out of the hemlock forest. Many big trees still stood on the edge of town, and some right in the center; and most of the houses were built of hemlock logs. There were a few, evidently belonging to Three Points' wealthier residents, that were massively built and patterned after the New England style of architecture.

There was no mistaking the tannery; the smell would have guided one there, even if the mountains of hemlock bark piled all about had not. Ramsay entered the long, low, shed-like building, and a man working at a steaming vat looked up curiously. Ramsay approached him with "Who's the boss man around here?"

"I am," an unseen man said.

Ramsay whirled to look at the man who had spoken, and he came face to face with Devil Chad.

CHAPTER THREE

ON THE BEACH

Ramsay felt an instant tension and a bristling anger, and he knew now that he should have connected two incidents. The man who had written to him and offered him a job in the Three Points tannery had signed his name 'Devlin Chadbourne.' Devlin Chadbourne—Devil Chad—and Ramsay took a backward step. Never before had he met a man so capable of arousing in him a cordial dislike that was almost an urge to start fighting immediately.

"Where's the *Holter*?" Devil Chad demanded.

"I sent her back to Milwaukee after Captain Schultz let me off here," Ramsay said sarcastically.

"Don't get smart with me, boy." Devil Chad glowered. "You was on the *Holter* when she sailed."

"Where were you?" Ramsay demanded.

"I'll ask the questions here!" Devil Chad's thick lips curled in an ugly oblong. "Where's the *Holter*?"

"At the bottom of Lake Michigan!" Ramsay flared. "Captain Schultz and one of your deck hands are lying drowned on the beach! I don't know where the others are."

Devil Chad's glass balls of eyes glinted. His face twisted into a horrible glare, and every inch of his big frame seemed to shrink and swell with the rage that consumed him. "You mean to tell me," he demanded furiously, "that all them hides was lost?"

"Men were lost," Ramsay pointed out.

"You mean to tell me," Devil Chad repeated, as though he had not heard Ramsay, "that all them hides was lost?"

"Swim out and get 'em," Ramsay invited. "I'll show you the place where I landed, and the *Holter* can't be more than a couple of miles out in the lake."

"What did Schultz do?" Devil Chad demanded.

"Drowned."

"You're pretty flip, boy," Devil Chad warned, "an' I don't put up with flip people. You tell me what happened."

"Your greasy tub was carrying one third more than ever should have been put on her, her equipment was no good, we ran into a storm and the engines quit."

"All them hides lost." Devil Chad was overwhelmed by this personal tragedy and could think of nothing else. "Couldn't you of done somethin'?"

"It wasn't my ship and they weren't my hides. What are you going to do for the families of the men who were lost?"

"Why should I do anything? They knew when they signed on that they was runnin' risks." Devil Chad turned his unreadable eyes squarely on Ramsay. "What do you want here?"

"Nothing."

"Ain't you the boy who wrote me from New York, an' asked me for a job?"

The man at the vat continued working and others stayed at their tasks, but Ramsay was aware of a rippling under-current. There was an uneasiness among the men, and a fear; and in spite of the fact that they kept busy they turned covert eyes on Ramsay and Devil Chad. The boy felt a flashing anger. Who was this man, and what was he, that so many others could live in almost craven fear of him?

"If you are," Devil Chad continued, still holding Ramsay in the cage of his eyes, "you can have the job but I hold back twenty-five cents a day until them hides are paid for."

"Take your job!" Ramsay exploded, "and go plumb to the bottom of the lake with it!"

"I warned you, boy," Devil Chad was talking softly now. "I warned you. I don't put up with flip people, an' now I'm goin' to teach you the lesson that I should of given you on the *Holter*."

"Why didn't you sail on the *Holter*?" Ramsay demanded.

Devil Chad made no answer. He was in a half-crouch, his huge head bent to his chest and his fists knotted so tightly that the knuckles were whitened. His shaggy hair tumbled forward on his forehead, and his eyes still held no expression.

Ramsay raised his voice so all in the building could hear. "You filthy pup! You lily-livered slug! You knew the *Holter* was going to the bottom some day! Even your deck hand knew it! You sent other men out to die, but didn't risk yourself! You haven't got enough money to hire me to work for you!"

Devil Chad was inching forward, his head still bent; and when he had advanced a foot, he sprang. It was the rush of a bull, but not a cumbersome bull. He flung out both arms, intending to crush Ramsay to his chest and break his ribs. It was the only way Devil Chad knew how to fight, but the boy knew other tricks.

When the bigger, heavier man launched his charge, Ramsay stood still. He saw those massive stretched arms, and knew their purpose, but he did not move until Devil Chad flung them out for his crushing embrace. Then, and only then, did Ramsay act.

He flitted aside, balancing himself on the balls of his feet and whirling even as he evaded the other's lunge. Like a snapping whip his clenched right fist flicked in to deliver a stinging blow to the side of his enemy's head. But the blow did little except spin Devil Chad around and arouse a mighty bellow in the depths of his enormous chest.

Ramsay remained poised, alert for the next charge, and an almost grim satisfaction drove other thoughts from his mind. He had not wanted this fight and had not forced it, but within him there was a curious feeling that it was fore-ordained, and now that it was here, he relished it. Devil Chad was not a man. He was an animal who thought as an animal thinks. Other men, other human beings, had lost their lives in his overloaded, unseaworthy ship, and all this brute could think of was the fact that he had lost his cargo.

Devil Chad's eyes, even in the heat of battle, remained opaque and strangely without expression. It was only his face, like a rubber mask expertly molded to form an expression of rage, that betrayed his fury. He swung heavily, running forward even as he launched his blow, and Ramsay ducked beneath it. He came up to land a hard left and a right on Devil Chad's jaw.

He might as well have struck a granite boulder. Devil Chad did not even flinch and the boy knew a moment's uncertainty. His enemy was a bull, but bulls were felled with pole-axes, not with fists. Ramsay backed lightly away.

All about now, knowing that Devil Chad was engrossed in the fight and had no time for them, men had openly stopped work and were staring at the battlers. On the faces of some was written incredulity. Some looked on with delighted interest, and an expectant smile lighted the swarthy features of a little Frenchman who had stopped moving cattle hides to watch Ramsay weave away from Devil Chad. There was no man here who, in some silent way, did not cheer the boy on, but there were none who expected him to win. All knew their master.

Devil Chad rushed again, swinging his fists like pistons as he did so, and again Ramsay side-stepped. He landed a fierce blow squarely on the other's nose and was gratified to see a crimson stream of blood spout forth to mingle darkly with his antagonist's black beard and mustache. A cold uncertainty rose within Ramsay.

He had fought before, many times, and he had defeated his opponents and had been defeated, but never before had he fought a man just like this one. Devil Chad, apparently, was able to absorb an endless amount of punishment with no effect whatever on himself. He was as tough as one of the trees that grew on the outskirts of Three Points.

Ramsay risked a fleeting backward glance to see where he was going, and edged away from the wall. He was breathing hard because of the tremendous physical effort he had exerted, but he was far from exhausted and he knew that, as long as he could keep the battle in the open, he could avoid the other's charges. But the certainty that he could not win this battle solidified. It seemed possible to pound Devil Chad all day long without hurting him at all.

"Kill him!" an excited man shouted.

Devil Chad paused just long enough to locate and identify this rash employee who dared encourage his enemy, and Ramsay felt a nausea in the pit of his stomach. When the battle ended, no matter who won, at least one man would have some explaining to do and probably a beating to take. The boy kept his eyes on Devil Chad, anticipating the other's next move.

Then he tripped over an unseen and unsuspected block of wood and fell backward.

Even as he fell he tried to pick himself up and scoot out of the way. But a bludgeon, the toe of Devil Chad's heavy boot, collided soddenly with his ribs and a sickening pain shot through his entire body. He turned, snatching furiously at the boot as it was raised again and still trying to wriggle away. His arm flipped convulsively as Devil Chad kicked him squarely on the wrist, and he felt a creeping numbness that began there and spread to his shoulder.

He rolled to escape his tormentor, rolled again, and struggled to his hands and knees. Vaguely, as though he were viewing it in some fantastic dream, he saw the big black boot flying at his head. The boot was a huge thing and so clearly-outlined that Ramsay saw every tiny wrinkle in it. He was aware of the stitching where the ponderous sole joined the upper leather, and he knew that he must get away. But that was a vague and misty thought, one he seemed unable to carry farther. A mighty rage flared within him.

No more than a split second elapsed before the boot struck, but it seemed like hours. Ramsay was aware of the fact that his two silver dollars, his last money, rolled out of his pockets and across the tannery's floor. A thousand colored lights danced in his head, and then he was back on the lake.

He had loved the lake, he remembered, and there was something wonderfully cool and refreshing about returning to it. A small boat with a crazy Dutch fisherman at her tiller danced out of the lake's gray stretches and sported gracefully before him. On top of the mast was a tame sea gull that clicked his mandibles and fluttered his wings. Ramsay even saw the boat's name written in fine script across her bows. She was the *Spray*.

The *Spray* hove to very close to Ramsay, and her skipper looked at him. He was a tall man, very powerful, and he was blond and easily laughing. There was no grimness about him, only grace and light spirit. Several men had gone sailing on a raft made of cattle hides, he told Ramsay, and they were in great trouble out on the lake. Did Ramsay care to go with him and help bring the unfortunates safely back? The sea gull, of course, would help too.

When Ramsay pretended not to hear, the crazy Dutch fisherman obligingly repeated his information. Again Ramsay pretended not to hear; whereupon the Dutch fisherman caught up a wooden bucket, dipped it into the lake and showered him with ice-cold water. He held the bucket waist-high, as though wondering whether more water was necessary, and the twinkle remained in his eyes and the laugh on his lips. It was impossible to be angry with him. Laughing back, Ramsay agreed to go help the foolish men who had sailed away on the cattle hides.

Then he awakened, to find a woman bathing his face with cold water.

For a moment she was a distorted picture, a hazy vision that advanced toward him and retreated far away. Again Ramsay almost lost himself in the dim world into which Devil Chad's boots had kicked him. The cold cloth on his face brought him back, and he opened his eyes to see the woman very clearly.

She was small, with a worn face, so weary from endless toil that the skin was drawn tightly over it. But her eyes were the brownest, the softest and the gentlest Ramsay had ever seen. Black hair was combed smoothly back on her head and caught in a knot at the base of her neck. Again she laid the cold cloth on his face, and the boy closed his eyes at the luxury of such a thing. Then he spoke, "Where am I?"

"*Sh-h.* Don't try to talk, M'sieu."

The woman, unmistakably French, rose and went into another room. Ramsay looked about him.

The room in which he lay was walled with rough, unplaned boards, and the ceiling was made of the same material. Only the floor, scrubbed so carefully that it glowed like a polished diamond, was of smooth boards. Light was admitted by a single small pane of glass, and the light reflected on a crucifix that hung on the far wall. There were a few pictures, yellow with age, a table over which a deer skin was gracefully draped, and a candle-holder with a half-burned candle. Everything was neat and spotlessly clean.

The woman came back bearing a hollowed-out gourd. She passed an arm around Ramsay's shoulders—despite her small size she was surprisingly strong—and assisted him to a half-sitting position. She held the gourd to his lips.

Ramsay drank deeply, and fell back sputtering. The gourd was partly-filled with cold water and partly with a whisky, so strong and violent that it burned his mouth and lips. He lay blinking, while tears welled in his eyes and flowed down his cheeks. The whisky, doubtless homemade, was strong enough to choke a horse. But, after a half-minute, it made itself felt. A warm glow spread from the roots of Ramsay's hair to the tips of his toes. Some of his many aches and pains lessened.

"More?" the woman inquired softly.

"Uh ... No—no thank you."

She put the gourd on the table and came over to lay a hand on his forehead. It was a calloused and work-hardened hand, but so gentle was she that her caress was scarcely a feather's touch. Ramsay smiled his thanks.

"How did I get here?" he asked again.

"My man, Pierre LeDou, he brought you. But now you must rest, M'sieu, and try to sleep. Badly have you been hurt."

The woman drew an exquisite, hand-sewn lace curtain, an incongruous thing in these rough surroundings, over the window, and semi-gloom reigned in the room. She tiptoed out, closing the door behind her, and Ramsay was left alone with his thoughts.

That mighty rage mounted within him again. He had been fighting with Devil Chad, he remembered, and not doing badly until he fell over some unseen object. Then he had been kicked into—into this. Experimentally Ramsay tried to move his legs, and found that he could do so. He clenched and unclenched his fists, and there in the half-light of an unknown room, in a stranger's house, he made a solemn vow. One day, no matter what else happened, he and Devil Chad would meet again. Devil Chad would pay, in full, for every twinge Ramsay suffered. In that moment Ramsay knew that he was not afraid.

His burning anger became tempered with pleasant wonder. This was a harsh land, but there was room for tenderness. He was a stranger and had been in Three Points only long enough to get himself kicked into insensibility, but there were those in Three Points who knew compassion and friendship. Otherwise, he would not now be lying in some unknown man's house and being ministered to by that man's wife. Pierre—Ramsay strove to recall the last name and could not. He fell into a quiet slumber.

The next time he awakened, the candle on his table was burning and his host—vaguely Ramsay remembered seeing him move hides about the tannery—was standing near. Like his wife, he was small and gentle, with a manner that belied the fierce little black mustache clinging to his upper lip. He was too small and gentle, Ramsay thought, ever to fit into a town such as Three Points. But certainly he was kind and good. He smiled, revealing flashing white teeth, and when he did Ramsay remembered the name, Pierre LeDou.

"How do you feel?" he asked briskly.

"Better." Ramsay grinned.

"He beat you," Pierre LeDou said. "*Sacre!* But he beat you!" The little man's eyes roved about the room, as though seeking the solution to a problem which he must solve, and Ramsay knew that he, too, hated Devil Chad. "He kicked you!" Pierre LeDou said.

"I know, and some day I'll pay him back for that."

Interest brightened in the little Frenchman's eyes. "You think so, M'sieu— M'sieu ..."

"Cartou," Ramsay said. "Ramsay Cartou. And I will not kill anybody unless I have to. But one day this Devil Chad will pay, ten times over, for everything he did to me."

"He is very hard man." Pierre LeDou sighed.

"So am I!" Ramsay gritted, and again anger rose within him. "Why should so many people tremble in their boots when he comes around?"

Pierre LeDou shrugged eloquently. "The job. A man has to have the job."

"I see. And Devil Chad controls 'the job'?"

"Not all," Pierre LeDou explained. "He does not walk so freely where the fishermen and farmers are."

"I'm beginning to like these fishermen and farmers more and more."

"They are nice," Pierre agreed, "but wild. Especially the fishermen. Oh, so wild! Out in the lake they go, afraid of nothing; but those that do not drown return with multitudes of fish."

"Do many drown?"

"Very many, but you cannot kill a fisherman. They say that the lake sends back two for every one it takes, and maybe that is so. At any rate, when a fisherman drowns, two more always appear. I would go fishing myself were it not that I am afraid. Are you hungry, M'sieu?"

"Yes," Ramsay answered frankly.

"Then I will get you something to eat."

Pierre LeDou disappeared. Ramsay lay back on the bed to think. Now this half-wild, half-tame country into which he had come was assuming a definite pattern. Some, like Pierre LeDou, had been attracted by the endless wealth offered, and had found only a back-breaking job with Devil Chad or his counterpart. Others, and Ramsay thought of Hans Van Doorst and Pieter Van Hooven, were finding wealth.

It was not wealth that could be measured in terms of money; probably the crazy Dutch fisherman and Pieter Van Hooven had little money, but just the same it was wealth. Rather than toil meekly for someone else and obey a master's every wish, they had chosen to discover for themselves the true richness of this endlessly rich land and they were discovering it. So some were afraid and some were not; and those who were not seemed to enjoy life at its fullest. And, as usual, there was the arrogant overlord, Devil Chad, who wanted everything for himself and who would take it if he could. He did not care what he did or whom he killed, as long as he got what he wanted.

Pierre LeDou came back, bearing a bowl on a wooden platter. Ramsay sniffed hungrily. The bowl was old and cracked, but like everything else in the house it was scrupulously clean, and the odors wafted from it would tempt the appetite of a dying man. Pierre put the bowl and a wooden spoon down where Ramsay could reach them, and Ramsay saw a meat stew in which fluffy dumplings floated.

"It is not much," the little Frenchman apologized. "Venison stew with dumplings, and that is all. Would you like some spirits to go with it?"

"Uh!" Ramsay remembered the fiery liquor. "No thanks. I would like some water."

"I can offer you milk."

"That will be fine."

Pierre disappeared, and returned with a bowl of milk and a beaker of the strong whisky. He gave the bowl to Ramsay and held the whisky aloft.

"Your health, M'sieu," he said.

He drained the beaker without even quivering, and Ramsay suppressed a shudder. Dipping the spoon in his venison stew, he tasted it. It was rich, with all the expertness of French cuisine behind it, and delicious. Ramsay took a chunk of venison in his mouth and chewed it with relish. Venison, fish and whatever else they could get out of the country doubtless meant much to the people who lived here.

"How long have you worked in the tannery?" he asked Pierre.

"Five years," the little Frenchman said. "Five long years. I shall work there much longer if God is kind."

"May He always be kind to you!" Ramsay said feelingly.

"My thanks to you, M'sieu Ramsay. And now, with your permission, I shall retire. I suggest that you sleep, for you look very weary. Should you want anything you have only to call."

Ramsay fell into a restful slumber from which he was awakened by the sound of people stirring. The early morning sun, just rising, caressed the curtained window softly and a sleepy bird twittered outside the window. There was the sound of lifted stove lids and of people stirring. Ramsay dozed off, then sprang guiltily awake and jumped out of bed.

He felt good, with only an occasional twinge of pain here and there. Hastily he pulled on his trousers and shirt, laced his shoes and smoothed his rumpled hair with his hand. When he had made himself as presentable as he could, he went into the other room.

Though the hour was still early and the sun not yet fairly up, Pierre LeDou had already left for his work in the tannery. His pleasant wife was pouring hot water from a pan on the stove into a big wooden bowl, evidently the receptacle in which dishes were washed. She turned around.

"Good morning!" Ramsay said cheerfully.

"Good morning, M'sieu." Then she cautioned him. "Should you be out of bed?"

"I feel fine." Ramsay grinned. "Strong as a bull and twice as hungry."

"Then I will prepare you something to eat. If M'sieu cares to do so, he may wash just outside the door."

"Thanks."

Ramsay went out the door. To one side, in front of the house, there was a big wooden bowl and two wooden pails filled with water. A well-worn trail threading away from the door obviously led to a well or spring. Hanging on a wooden peg driven into a hole, drilled in the cabin's wall, were a clean towel and washcloth. Even the door's hinges, cleverly carved pins that turned on holes drilled into wooden blocks attached to the cabin's wall, were wood. Evidently, in this country, wood substituted for metal.

Ramsay filled the bowl with water, washed himself and went back into the cabin. Pierre LeDou's wife was bending over a skillet from which came the smell of frying fish. Ramsay sniffed hungrily, and licked his lips. She turned the fish, let it cook a little while longer, and put it on the table, along with feather-light biscuits, butter and cold milk. Ramsay ate hungrily, but tried to curb his appetite so he would also eat decently, and as he ate he talked.

"Why," he asked Pierre LeDou's wife, "did your husband bring me here?"

"You were hurt and needed help," she said simply.

In sudden haste Ramsay felt his pocket, and discovered that the two silver dollars were gone. He remembered that he had lost them while he fought with Devil Chad, and a flood of embarrassment almost overwhelmed him.

"I—I have no money to pay you," he said awkwardly.

For the first time she looked reprovingly at him. "We did not ask for money, M'sieu. One does not."

Ramsay knew another awkward moment and a little shame. "It is very good of you," he said.

She said, "One does not neglect a fellow human."

Ramsay finished eating and pushed his dishes back. Pierre LeDou's wife, who had already finished washing the rest of the dishes, put Ramsay's in the dish water and left them there. She smiled at him. "It would be well if you rested."

"I'm not tired. Really I'm not."

"You should rest. Badly were you hurt."

"Let me sit here a while."

"As long as you sit."

She went to a cupboard and took from it a big ball of strong linen thread. From the table she caught up a small board. Wrapping the thread twice around the board, she knotted it. Slipping the thread from the board, she hung the loop she had made on a wooden peg and made a new loop. Her hands flew so swiftly that in a few moments she had seventeen of the meshes, all joined together.

"What are you doing?" Ramsay inquired interestedly.

"Making a gill net," she explained. "It was ordered by Baptiste LeClair, a fisherman, and is to have a four and a half-inch mesh. So we use a mesh board that is exactly two and a quarter inches wide and wrap the thread twice around. Now I have seventeen. See?"

"I see."

She strung the seventeen meshes on a wooden rod, placed two chairs far enough apart so that the meshes stretched, tied the rod to them and began knitting on the net she had started. "The net is to be seventeen meshes, or seventy-six and one-half inches, wide. Now I lengthen it."

Under the boy's interested eyes the gill net grew swiftly, and as it lengthened she wrapped it around the rod. Ramsay watched every move. "How long will it be?" he queried.

"One net," she told him, "is about two hundred and fifty feet long. But usually several are tied together to form a box of nets. A box is about fourteen hundred feet."

"Isn't that a lot?"

She smiled. "A crew of three good men, like Hans Van Doorst or Baptiste LeClair, with a good Mackinaw boat can handle two boxes."

"Could you make this net longer if you wished to?"

"Oh, yes. It could be many miles long. Two hundred and fifty feet is a good length for one net because, if it is torn by strong water or heavy fish, it may be untied and repaired while the rest may still be used."

"What else must you do?"

"After the net is two hundred and fifty feet long, I will use fifteen- or sixteen-thread twine through from three to six meshes on the outer edge. This, in turn, will be tied to ninety-thread twine which extends the full length."

Ramsay was amazed at the way this quiet little woman reeled off these figures, as though she were reciting a well-learned lesson. But he wanted to know even more. "How do they set such a net?"

"The fishermen gather small, flat stones, about three to the pound, and cut a groove around them so that they can be suspended from a rope. These are called sinkers, and are tied to the net about nine feet apart. For floats they use cedar blocks, about two feet long by one-quarter of an inch thick and an inch and a quarter wide. They bore a small hole one inch from the end, then split the block to the bored hole. The floats—and the number they use depends on the depth to which they sink the net—are pushed over the ninety-thread twine."

"Let me try!" Ramsay was beginning to feel the effects of idleness and wanted action.

"But of course, M'sieu."

Ramsay took the mesh board in his hand and, as he had seen her do, wrapped the thread twice around it. But, though it had looked simple when she did it, there was a distinct knack to doing it right. The mesh board slipped from his fingers and the twine unwound. Madame LeDou laughed. "Let me show you."

Patiently, carefully, she guided his fingers through the knitting of a mesh, then another and a third and fourth. Ramsay felt a rising elation. He had liked the *Spray* when he saw her and now he liked this. Fishing, from the making of the nets to setting them, seemed more than ever a craft that was almost an art. He knitted a row of meshes across the gill net, and happily surveyed his work.

At the same time he remained aware of the fact that she could knit three times as fast as he. Ramsay thrust his tongue into his cheek and grimly continued at his work.

After an hour Madame LeDou said soberly, "You do right well, M'sieu. But should you not rest now?"

Ramsay said, "This is fun."

"It is well that you enjoy yourself. Would you consider it uncivil if I left you for a while?"

"Please do what you must."

She left, and Ramsay continued to work on the net. As he did, his skill improved. Though he was still unable to knit as swiftly as Madame LeDou, he could make a good net. And there was a feel, a tension, to the thread. Within itself the thread had life and being. It was supple, strong and would not fail a fisherman who depended upon it.

Madame LeDou returned, smiled at him and went unobtrusively about the task of preparing a lunch. So absorbed was he in his net-making that he scarcely tasted the food. All afternoon he worked on the net.

Madame LeDou said approvingly, "You make a good net, M'sieu. You have knitted almost four pounds of thread into this one. The most skilled net-makers, those who have had years of experience, cannot knit more than six or seven pounds in one day."

Twilight shadows were lengthening when Pierre LeDou returned. The little man, as always, was courteous. But behind his inherited Gallic grace and manners lay a troubled under-current. Pierre spoke in rapid French to his wife, and she turned worried eyes on their guest. Ramsay stopped knitting the net.

All afternoon there had been growing upon him an awareness that he could not continue indefinitely to accept the LeDou's hospitality, and now he knew that he must go. The pattern had definite shape, and the reason behind Pierre's uneasiness was not hard to fathom. Devil Chad was the ruler, and Devil Chad must rule. Who harbored his enemy must be his enemy, and Pierre LeDou needed the job in the tannery. Should he lose it, the LeDous could not live.

With an air of spontaneity, anxious not to cause his host and hostess any embarrassment, Ramsay rose and smiled. "It has been a most enjoyable stay at your home," he said. "But of course it cannot continue. I have work to find. If you will be kind enough to shelter me again tonight, I will go tomorrow, and I shall never forget the LeDous."

CHAPTER FOUR

TROUBLE FOR THE SPRAY

Early the next morning, when Pierre departed for work, Ramsay bade farewell to Madame LeDou and left their house with his kind host. He did so with a little reluctance, now that all his money was gone and the future loomed more uncertainly than ever. At the same time there was about him a rising eagerness and an unfulfilled expectation.

It seemed to him that, since swimming ashore from the sinking *Holter*, he had ceased to be a boy and had become a man. And a man must know that all desirable things had their undesirable aspects. This country was wonderful. If, to stay in it, he must come to grips with other men—men as strong and as cruel as Devil Chad—and with nature too, Ramsay felt himself willing to do that.

As soon as the two were fifty yards from the LeDou home he purposely dropped behind Pierre and leaned against a huge hemlock until the little man was out of sight. Pierre had said nothing and Ramsay had not asked, but the latter knew Devil Chad had told the Frenchman that, if he valued his job in the tannery, he must no longer shelter Ramsay. The boy had no wish to further embarrass his host or to jeopardize his job by being seen with him. Therefore he leaned against the tree until Pierre had had time to reach and enter the tannery.

Slowly Ramsay left his tree and walked down the same path that Pierre had followed. Badly as he needed a job, it was useless to try to get one in the tannery. He slowed his pace even more as he walked past the building. He had been beaten by Devil Chad, and he might be beaten a second time should they fight again; but he was not afraid to try. His body had been hurt, but not his courage.

Almost insolently Ramsay stopped where he could be seen from the tannery's open door, and waited there. He was aware of curious, half-embarrassed glances from men hurrying into the place, and then they avoided looking at him. Finally a man stopped. He spoke to a man who halted beside him.

"All right, Jules. Get in an' start to work."

He was a straw boss or foreman, Ramsay decided, and his voice betrayed his New England forebears. An older man, with hair completely gray, like all the rest he was wrinkled and weathered. Physically he was lean and tough, but he did not seem belligerent or even unkind. When the last worker had entered the tannery, he turned to Ramsay.

"You needn't be afraid, son. Mr. Chadbourne went to Milwaukee last night."

"I'm not afraid. I was just wondering if he wouldn't come out for a second start."

"Look, son," the other's air was that of an older and wiser person trying to reason with an impetuous boy, "you haven't got a chance. The best thing you can do is get out of town before Mr. Chadbourne comes back."

"Maybe I like this town."

"You can only cause trouble by staying here."

"I've been in trouble before, too."

The older man shrugged, as though he had discharged his full responsibility in warning Ramsay, and said, "It's your funeral, my boy. Stay away from the tannery."

"You needn't worry."

Ramsay strolled on down the dusty street, and in spite of himself he was a little relieved. If Devil Chad had gone to Milwaukee, probably to arrange for another shipload of hides, it was unlikely that he would be back before night at the earliest. Ramsay would not have to fight again today; presumably he was free to do as he pleased without any fear of interruption. He thrust his hands into empty pockets and, to cheer himself up, started to whistle.

A fat Indian, dressed in ragged trousers, which some white man had thrown out, and an equally-tattered black coat which he could not button across his immense, naked stomach, grinned at him. Ramsay grinned back and winked. His friends in New York had been awe-stricken at the very thought of venturing into the wild Midwest where, they thought, scalping parties occurred every few hours and no white man was safe from the savages. Ramsay had enjoyed himself by elaborating on the part he would play when such a war party came along. But he had discovered for himself, before he left Chicago, that the Indians in this section of Wisconsin were harmless. When they could they sold bead work and basketry to the settlers and they were not above stealing. But they were not warlike.

Ramsay strode past another building, a big one with two separate floors and an attic. Its chimney belched smoke, and from within came the whine of saws and other machinery. In front of the building were stacked a great number of barrels, made of white pine and with hoops formed from the black ash tree. Ramsay hesitated a moment and entered.

Three Points was obviously a raw frontier town, but definitely it was not as raw as Ramsay had expected it to be. Obviously there was at least one industrial plant in addition to the tannery. It seemed to be a cooper's shop, engaged in the production of barrels, and it might hold a job for him. He stopped just inside the door, trying to adjust his ears to the scream of a big circular saw that was powered by a steam engine. Beyond were lathes and various other machines, and a great many wooden pails were piled against the far wall. This factory, then, made both barrels and pails.

Presently a middle-aged man, with the neatest clothing Ramsay had yet seen in Three Points, came out of an office and walked toward him. He shouted to make himself heard above the screaming saw, "Yes?"

"Are you the manager here?" Ramsay shouted back.

"Yes."

"Need any men?"

"What?"

Ramsay grinned faintly. The factory, if not bedlam, was close to it. It was incredible that anyone at all could carry on an intelligent, or even an intelligible, conversation inside it. Ramsay shouted, "Let's go outside!"

The other followed him out, and far enough from the door so they could hear each other. Ramsay turned to his companion, "My name's Ramsay Cartou and I'm looking for a job. Do you have any to offer?"

The manager looked soberly at Ramsay's battered face, then with the toe of his shoe he began tracing a circle in the dirt. He hesitated. Then, "I'm afraid not."

Ramsay felt a stirring anger. Definitely there was more work in Three Points than there were men to do it. The town had need of strong workers. For a moment he looked steadily at the manager, who looked away. Then he swallowed and tried a new tack, "What do you do with all the barrels?"

"Most of them go to fishermen who use them to ship their catches to Chicago. The pails are shipped by boat to wherever there is a market for them."

"And you can't give me a job?"

"That's right."

"Why?" Ramsay challenged.

"We—we have a full crew."

"I see. Now will you answer one question?"

"Certainly."

"Does 'Mister' Chadbourne own this place too?"

"He has a financial interest ..." The other stopped short. "See here, young man! I have told you that I cannot offer you a job and that should be sufficient!"

"I just wanted to know why," Ramsay said.

He turned and walked away from the cooper's shop. His chin was high, and anger seethed within him. Devil Chad, apparently, owned most of Three Points and a lot of other things between that and Milwaukee. If there was an opportunity to earn a dollar, honest or dishonest, Devil Chad was seizing that opportunity. Obviously the manager of the cooper's shop had heard of his fight with Ramsay—in a small community like this everyone would have heard of it—and was afraid to give him a job. Ramsay resumed his tuneless whistling.

Plainly he was going to get nowhere in Three Points. But definitely he had no intention of running away with his tail between his legs, like a whipped puppy. He liked this lakeshore country and he intended to stay in it. If he had to fight to do that, then he would fight.

Between the rugged trunks of tall hemlock trees he caught a glimpse of the lake, sparkling blue in the sunshine and gently ruffled by a soft south wind. He turned his steps toward it, and now he walked eagerly. The lake was magic, a world in itself which never had been tamed and never would be tamed. He shivered ecstatically. This was what he had come west to find. Devil Chad and his tannery, the town of Three Points, and even Milwaukee paled into nothingness when compared to the lake. He broke from the last trees and saw Lake Michigan clearly.

A heavy wooden pier extended out onto it, and a sailing vessel was tied up at one side. Ramsay read her name. She was the *Brilliant*, from Ludington, Michigan, and a line of men were toiling up a gangplank with heavy bags which they were stacking on the pier. On the pier's other side a steamer, a side-wheeler like the *Holter*, was loading leather from Devil Chad's tannery. She was the *Jackson*, a freighter that carried assorted cargoes between Three Points, Milwaukee and Chicago.

Ramsay strolled out on the pier and brightened when the cold lake air struck his face. It was impossible to be on the lake, or near it, and feel stolid or dull. It provided its own freshness, and Ramsay thought it also furnished a constant inspiration. He watched the sweating men continue to bring loaded bags up from the sailing vessel and approached near enough to ask a burly deck hand, "What's this cargo?"

The man looked surlily at him. "What's it look like?"

"Diamonds." Ramsay grinned.

"Well, it ain't. It's salt."

"What the blazes will anyone do with so much salt?"

"Eat it," the deck hand grunted. "People hereabouts like salt." Then he, too, grinned. "Naw, it's for fishermen. They got to have somethin' to salt their catches in."

"Oh. I see."

Ramsay added this bit of information to the lore he had already gathered. Obviously fishing consisted of more than just catching fish. Actually taking the fish, of course, was the most exciting and romantic part. But the fishermen could not ply their trade at all without women like Madame LeDou who made their nets, a shop like the Three Points' cooper's shop which provided the barrels into which the fish were packed, or vessels like the *Brilliant* which brought salt that kept the fish from spoiling.

Ramsay stayed on the pier until the *Brilliant* was unloaded, and licked his lips while he watched her crew eating thick sandwiches. They took a whole loaf of bread, sliced it lengthwise, packed the center with meat, cheese, fish and anything else they could lay their hands on, and, according to their taste, washed it down with cold lake water or beakers of whisky. Ramsay looked away.

Madame LeDou had provided him with a substantial breakfast, but this was an invigorating country wherein one soon became hungry again. Ramsay patted his empty stomach.

Probably Madame LeDou would give him something to eat should he go back there, but he had already posed enough problems for the LeDous. Besides, he did not like the idea of asking for food. He left the pier to walk past the Lake House, Three Points' only hotel. Savory odors of cooking food wafted to his nostrils and made him drool. He walked past the Lake House, then turned to walk back. He trotted up the steps and sat down at a table spread with a white cloth.

A hard-eyed woman, wearing a brown dress over which she had tied a neat white apron, came up to him. Ramsay leaned back. He had decided to make his play, and he might as well play it to the end.

"What does the menu offer?" he asked almost haughtily.

"Whitefish at fifteen cents, venison at fifteen cents, a boiled dinner at ten cents."

"What? No steak?"

"The steak dinner," the woman said, "costs thirty cents. With it you get potatoes, coffee, salad and apple pie."

"Bring it to me," Ramsay said. "And please be prompt. My time is valuable."

"As soon as possible," the woman said.

Ramsay relaxed in his chair. A half-hour later the waitress brought him a broiled sirloin, so big that it overflowed the platter on which it rested. There were crisp fried potatoes, coffee—a rare beverage in this country—cream, a salad and a huge wedge of apple pie. Ramsay ate hungrily, then the waitress approached him.

"Will you pay now?"

"It is a lot," said Ramsay, who could not have swallowed another crust, "to pay for such a puny meal."

"I told you the price before you ordered."

"It doesn't matter," Ramsay waved a languid hand. "Especially since I have no money. What do we do now?"

Ramsay stood in the kitchen of the Lake House, and by the light of an oil lamp piled the last of what had been a mountain of dishes, into warm water. There must, he thought, have been thousands of them, but there were only a few more and he dropped one of those. Instantly the woman who had served him popped into the kitchen.

"Must you be so clumsy?"

"It is the only dish I have broken out of all I have washed," Ramsay said. "Don't you think I have paid off my dinner by this time?"

"You knew the price before you ordered."

"The way you've had me working since, I earned the whole cow. Haven't I repaid you, with perhaps a bonus of a sandwich for supper?"

"Sit down, kid," the woman said gruffly.

She brought him a sandwich, huge slices of fluffy homemade bread between which thick slices of beef nestled, and a bowl of milk. Ramsay ate hungrily, and after he had finished his hostess talked to him. "You're the youngster Devil Chad beat up, aren't you?"

"I tripped," Ramsay said grimly.

"Devil Chad trips 'em all. You're crazy if you think you can get away with anything. Best thing you can do is leave."

Ramsay said, "I guess I'm just naturally crazy."

The woman shrugged. "I'm tellin' you for your own good, kid. You'll get nowhere in Three Points as long as Chad don't like you. Why not be a smart little boy and beat it back to wherever you came from?"

Ramsay said, "That isn't a good idea."

"You're a stubborn kid, ain't you?"

"Mule-headed," Ramsay agreed. "Even worse than a mule."

"Well, if you won't take good advice, there's not much I can do. Would you like to sleep here tonight?"

"Nope. I'll be going now, and thanks for the steak."

"Well ... Good luck, kid."

"Thanks."

Ramsay walked out into the darkness and drew his jacket tightly about him. The lake shore was cold by day, much colder by night when there was no sun to warm it. He had brought extra clothing, but all his personal belongings had gone down with the *Holter*. He looked dismally at the dark town—Three Points seemed to go to bed with the setting sun—and wandered forlornly down toward the lake front. Both the sailing vessel from Ludington and the *Jackson* were gone.

A little wind was driving wavelets gently against the shore, and the lap-lap of their rising and falling made pleasant music in the night. Ramsay wandered out on the pier, where the stacked bags of salt were covered with tarpaulins. He looked furtively around.

Nobody else was on or even near the pier, and it seemed unlikely that anyone would come. He curled up close to the bags of salt and drew the flowing end of a tarpaulin over his body. He pillowed his head on a protruding bag and snuggled very near to the stack.

The pier was hard, but he had slept on hard beds before and the barrier of salt broke the wind's force. The tarpaulin, of heavy duck, made a warm blanket. In spite of the odds he faced, Ramsay felt a wonderful sense of well-being and peace. He went quietly to sleep.

When he awakened, soft gray dawn was stealing like a fawn out of the summer sky. Three Points, not yet awake, slumbered in the dim morning. Ramsay crawled out from beneath the tarpaulin and rose to look at the town.

Nobody gave up any battles; but nobody knocked his head against a stone wall or strove against hopeless odds. Even the little black horse had not done that. He might just as well see things as they were. Devil Chad ruled Three Points and, with his present resources, Ramsay could not fight Devil Chad. But it was certain that Chad could not rule all of Milwaukee, too, and Milwaukee would need workers. He could go back there, get a job and plan his future after he had it.

A sudden inspiration seemed to fall right out of the brightening sky.

The Van Hoovens! Pieter Van Hooven had told him to come back should he fail to find what he expected in Three Points, and Pierre LeDou had assured him that Devil Chad did not walk so freely among the farmers and fishermen. Maybe Pieter could give him a job, at least something that would offer security until he was able to get himself oriented; and if he could, Ramsay wanted to stay in this part of the country. It was better than Milwaukee.

Briskly he left the pier and struck down the sand beach. Now that he had decided to take this step, he felt lighter and happier. Maybe he would and maybe he would not have liked working in the tannery, even if that had been ruled by some other man than Devil Chad, but he knew that he would like the Van Hoovens and their way of life.

He moved fast, staying far enough up on the beach so he need not step in wet sand but near enough the water so he could walk on sun-baked sand over which high water had already rolled. That was packed hard, almost to the consistency of concrete.

The sun was well up when he came again to the Van Hooven's pleasant home. Resolutely he walked up and knocked on the back door.

A second later it opened, and Marta Van Hooven flashed a warm smile of welcome. "Oh! Come in."

Pieter, who had already finished his milking and was now seated at the breakfast table, said, "Hello."

"Hello," Ramsay said. "I thought I'd stop in and see you on ..." He fumbled. "On my way back to Milwaukee."

Pieter looked seriously at him. "You're not going to work in Three Points?"

"No," Ramsay said bluntly. "Mr. Chadbourne and I did not see eye to eye. In fact, three minutes after we met our fists were flying in each other's eyes."

"You fought Devil Chad?"

"I did, and got well-beaten."

Pieter said quietly, "Some day somebody will kill him."

"Some day somebody might."

"Eat," Pieter invited. He pushed a platter of eggs at the boy and forked a thick slice of home-cured ham onto his plate. Then he placed the dish of yellow butter where Ramsay could help himself and put a plate of feather-light fresh-baked rolls where he was able to reach it. Marta came softly in from the kitchen with a bowl of cold milk.

Ramsay ate, primly at first, then gave way to his enormous appetite. Pieter served him another slice of ham. The boy took two more eggs and another roll, which he spread lavishly with butter. Sighing, unable to swallow another crumb, he pushed his plate back. Pieter looked gravely at him. "Do you have to go to Milwaukee?"

"No, I just thought I might find a job there."

"You can," Pieter assured him. "But if a job is what you want, a job is what I can give you. I can't pay you any money, at least until we have sold our fall crops, because we haven't any. But I can give you all you can eat, a good bed to sleep in, and I have some clothes that will fit you."

Ramsay said deliberately, "Devil Chad won't like you for that."

"Around here," and there was no air of braggadocio in Pieter's words, "we don't much care what Devil Chad likes."

Ramsay looked hard at his host, and then the two young men grinned at each other.

"You've got yourself a man," Ramsay said. "What do we do first?"

Hidden from the house by a jutting shoulder of land, Ramsay stood beside the small lake on Pieter Van Hooven's property and peeled off his clothes. All day long, interrupted in mid-morning by Marta, who brought him a substantial lunch, at noon by a huge and delicious dinner and again in mid-afternoon with a lunch, he had toiled in Pieter Van Hooven's sprouting corn.

All day long the sun had beaten down and, though the lake shore was cool enough, a man doing hard physical labor could easily work up a sweat. But it was good. Ramsay had felt the sun's rays penetrate to and warm the very marrow of his bones. In spite of the hard labor he had been doing, few times in his life had he felt as agile and supple and wholly alive as this.

He plunged headlong into the lake and came up gasping. The water was cold, though not nearly as cold as the big lake; and after Ramsay's body was adjusted to it, a delicious glow ran through his whole physical being. He dived again, then climbed up on the soft grass to let the lowering sun dry him before he put his clothes on.

He dressed slowly, happily, and now all his cares were behind him. This was the place for him, and no longer did he have the slightest doubt that he was going to like everything about it. Fresh and vigorous, the day's toil washed away, he walked slowly down to Lake Michigan and stared across it. Supper in half an hour, Pieter had said when he had advised Ramsay to stop work and have a swim, and no more than half that time had elapsed. The rest could profitably be spent in just looking at this endlessly fascinating water.

Ramsay stared across the lake. More than ever it seemed a live creature and one of many moods. Ramsay had seen it roaring-mad, and now he saw it gentle as a lamb. There was scarcely a ripple anywhere. Absorbed in the lake, Ramsay was aware of nothing else until a horse snorted very close to him. When he whirled, he knew that he had seen the same horse and rider before.

It was the body-watcher, Joe Mannis, and he was riding the black-and-white horse which he had ridden when he had warned Ramsay away from the drowned Captain Schultz and the deck hand. The huge cowboy hat tilted precariously on his head and the blue jeans, apparently unwashed in a good many months, clung tightly to his legs. Thick black hair escaped from beneath the hat, and he looked Ramsay up and down. "What are you doin' here?"

"What's it to you?"

"Well, nothin' I expect. Nothin' at all. But just don't bother me again when I'm workin' at my trade."

"I won't," Ramsay promised, "unless I have a couple of pistols, too."

"Just don't bother me when I'm workin' at my trade," the other repeated, "an' we'll get along fine."

"You think so?" Ramsay snapped.

Missing the challenge implied in Ramsay's words, Joe Mannis trotted his horse up the sand beach toward Three Points. Ramsay looked without interest at his retreating back. Joe Mannis was an unsavory man, he decided, but unlike Devil Chad, he was a stupid man. Only when backed by his pistols would Joe be much of a threat.

Ramsay pushed his drying hair back with his hands and went around to the rear of the Van Hooven house. That was also a custom, it seemed. Formal visitors, if there were any, might enter by the front door; but everyone else went around to the rear. Obviously the visitor who had arrived while Ramsay bathed and stood on the shore, was not formal.

He was a tall, gaunt man with a thin face and a hooked nose. Except for a white shirt, the collar of which was adorned by a bright ribbon that could hardly be called a tie, from his stovepipe hat to his shoes he was dressed entirely in black. An outlandish rig, a four-wheeled cart with a fringed top supported on four posts, stood in the yard. Its curtains were rolled up, and the cart seemed to contain everything from wash tubs to pins. Pieter and the stranger were unhitching a gray horse that stood patiently between the cart's shafts.

Pieter called the boy over, "Ramsay, this is Mr. Hammersly."

Mr. Hammersly, so-called, turned and thrust forth a huge hand. "Tradin' Jack," he amended. "Tradin' Jack Hammersly. You need anythin', I got it. Fairer prices as you'll find in Three Points, Chicago, or Milwaukee. Need a box of candy for that girl of yours, Ramsay?"

"I haven't any girl," Ramsay said.

"You'll have one," Tradin' Jack declared. "Every young buck like you needs a pert doe. Can't get along without 'em, I always say. Yup, you'll have one. When you get one, remember Tradin' Jack."

"I will," Ramsay promised.

While Tradin' Jack washed up at the stand beside the back door, Pieter led the gray horse to the barn, stripped it of its harness and loosed it with the little black horse. The two animals touched friendly noses.

Pieter returned, and all three went in to the groaning table which Marta had ready. It seemed a natural thing here, Ramsay observed, to expect all passing wayfarers to share whatever there was to be had. Gracefully Tradin' Jack lifted the tails of his long black coat and sat down.

"Left Milwaukee day before yesterday," he said. "Stopped off to see the Blounts, down at Blounts' Landin'...."

Marta and Pieter Van Hooven gave rapt attention, and even Ramsay found himself interested. Aside from being a trader, it appeared that Tradin' Jack Hammersly was also a walking newspaper. He knew everything about everybody between Three Points and Milwaukee, and between Milwaukee and Kenosha. Endlessly he related tales of new babies, new weddings and new engagements. Tradin' Jack knew that Wilhelm Schmidt's horse had the colic but probably would recover, and that Mrs. Darmstedt, that would be the wife of Pete Darmstedt, had shot a black bear right in her own front yard.

There was nothing about the people he did not know and not much that he was unwilling to tell. Finished, he got down to business. "Any eggs for me, Marta?"

"Twenty dozen," she said, "all fresh."

"Fourteen cents a dozen," Tradin' Jack said promptly.

"Yaah," Marta, too, was bargaining now, "I can get that in Three Points."

"Take it in trade an' I'll allow you fifteen," Tradin' Jack said. "Got to keep my customers sweet."

Before he went to bed Tradin' Jack arranged with Pieter to have a butchered pig ready for him when he returned from Three Points the day after tomorrow. Two and a half cents a pound he would pay, or two and three-quarters if Pieter would take it in trade. He left with the Van Hoovens a tempting array of calico, ribbons, needles, pins, a new axe and hammer, a box of nails and other things which were always useful and always needed.

The next morning Ramsay roused himself out of bed at dawn to find Tradin' Jack already gone. He had sensed the storm that was approaching, Pieter said, and, if possible, he wanted to get into Three Points before it struck. Ramsay felt a strange uneasiness and an unrest. Going outside, he saw that yesterday's blue skies had given way to ominous masses of gray clouds. His uneasiness mounted.

Something terrible was being brewed within the giant lake, and shortly it would erupt. A strong wind sent high waves leaping up onto the shore. They fell back, only to be replaced with more waves. Ramsay shuddered.

If there was terror in this, there was also grandeur. The lake, angered, was a fearful and wonderful spectacle. It was a gargantuan thing which seemed to writhe in an agony which, somehow, was created by itself. A few drops of rain pattered down. The wind blew harder.

Pieter and Ramsay went to the barn to repair tools, and neither spoke as they stared through the barn's open door. The waves were raging now, launching endless attacks on the shore and always rolling back.

Suddenly Ramsay leaped to his feet and stifled a cry. Far out in the lake's surging gray masses he thought that he had seen something pure white. But he could not be sure. A moment later he saw it again. A sail! Then he was able clearly to identify a little peanut shell of a boat.

She was the *Spray*, and she was in serious trouble.

CHAPTER FIVE

RESCUE

A fresh gust of wind sent the waves leaping higher, and for a moment only the furious lake could be seen. Ramsay rose, and Pieter rose beside him; and both went to the barn door. They stood alert, still not speaking and not even certain of what they had seen. Then they saw it again.

Beyond any possible doubt it was the *Spray*, and she was working valiantly to get into shore. Ramsay swallowed a lump in his throat. He had first seen the *Spray* as a dancing bit of gaiety on a lake as stormy as this one, and then she had seemed so sure of herself and so capable. Now she was like a shot-wounded duck which, no longer able to rise in graceful flight, must lie on the water and flutter desperate wings. For another tense moment Ramsay and Pieter stood side by side.

By inches the *Spray* was fighting her way toward shore, but a glance was sufficient to reveal the tremendous odds against her ever making safety. Still, even in this terrible dilemma, there was a spirit about her which the *Holter* never had and never could have. The two men on the *Spray*—and did not the crazy Dutch fisherman usually carry a crew of four?—seemed to be working calmly and easily. There was, from this distance, no trace of the near-panic that had reigned when the *Holter* went down.

Ramsay knew a moment's intense gratification. This was part of the dream, part of the picture he had engraved in his heart when he first saw the *Spray* and her skipper. When they challenged the lake, they accepted it in all its aspects. Now they were behaving as all fishermen should behave. Before they could even begin to follow their trade they must make an unbreakable pact with their fortune on the water, be it good or bad.

Then the trance was broken. Out on the lake, within sight of Pieter and Ramsay, men were about to die. They must not die if there was any way to help them. As though their eyes were guided by one common impulse, both men looked toward Pieter's small boat.

It was a clumsy craft, strongly-built of heavy timbers which Pieter himself had hand-sawed in his spare time. Usually, when Pieter wasn't using the boat, it was pulled high enough on the beach so storm-driven battering rams of waves could not touch it, and so it was now. Side by side, with no need to speak, Pieter and Ramsay left the barn and raced toward the boat.

Wind-driven rain soaked their clothing before they had gone ten feet, but they paid no attention to it. Kneeling, one on either side of the fourteen-foot boat, they strove to push it back into the lake. Pieter shouted to make himself heard above the roar of the wind and the smashing waves. "Wait!"

Ramsay stopped pushing while Pieter took the long oars out of their locks and laid them lengthwise in the boat. The boy nodded approvingly. As things were, it seemed all but impossible to launch the boat. If they launched it and lost an oar in the high seas, they were doomed to disaster, anyhow.

"Now!" Pieter shouted.

The boat scraped a deep furrow in the wet sand as, with a concerted effort, they pushed it backwards. Not looking at the savage combers, Ramsay gave all his attention to the boat. They would have to work with all possible speed to get it into the lake and the oars in place, because the waves were rising to enormous heights now. He felt the boat's square stern touch water.

Then an irresistible giant, a force that would bear no interference, took hold and shoved the little craft almost as far up on the beach as it had been when they tried to launch it. Leaving the boat half-filled with water, the smashing wave washed away from the wet sand.

Ramsay stood erect to catch his breath. They had given all their strength to backing the boat into the lake, and as they were about to succeed it had been plucked from their hands as easily as a strong man might snatch a flower from the hands of a baby. He glanced out across the water to assure himself that the *Spray* was still floating, then looked desperately at Pieter.

"Nose first!" Pieter said. "Turn it around!"

He shouted to make himself heard, but there was about him an almost maddening calmness as he worked. Ramsay restrained his impatience. They must not lose a second's time; but if they were going to do this at all, it must be done exactly right. Both on one side of the boat, they raised it to let the water spill out.

In spite of his drenched clothing and the cold air that blew in from the lake, Ramsay was sweating. Pieter's boat had been built by a farmer, not a fisherman. It was all right on a calm day when Pieter wanted to go fishing, but certainly it had never been built to weather storms. So heavy was the craft that the combined strength of two men was needed to tip the water from it.

They let the boat drop heavily back on its side, and the oars fell out. Still calmly, refusing to become excited, Pieter picked them up and placed them in the oar locks. Again Ramsay understood. Both men knew this for a furious storm but both had underestimated its fury. At the best, should they be able to get the boat into the lake, they would have a split second to float her and the oars had to be ready. It was better to take a chance on losing an oar than to have the boat driven back onto the beach.

Kneeling, Ramsay felt his muscles stand out like stretched cords as he gave every ounce of strength to turning the boat around. He was sweating again—and short of breath. Only the pressing urgency and the great need for immediate action gave him the strength to continue.

Then the craft seemed to move a little easier, and Ramsay glanced around to see Marta working beside them. Noting them from the house, and understanding their mission, she had thrown a shawl about her shoulders and raced out to help. With almost maddening slowness the boat turned until its curved nose faced the lake.

Ramsay on one side and Pieter on the other slid it down the wet sand toward the water. The boy bit his lip fiercely to help keep control of himself. Nothing must go amiss here, and a wrong or panic-stricken move could mean disaster. Because this launching demanded machine-like precision, Ramsay fought to control the fire in his brain. Carefully he thought out each exact step.

Get the boat into the lake until it floated. Then leap in beside Pieter, grab an oar and time his strokes to Pieter's. Fight their way out to the stricken *Spray* and rescue those aboard her.

It seemed a simple matter, but never before in his whole life had Ramsay faced anything more complex. It couldn't be done, his mind said, while at the same time something else told him that it could and must be done. He glanced around and curiously, as though the picture were registering somewhere other than in his own eyes, he saw Marta Van Hooven.

She was standing at the edge of the lake, her dress and shawl sodden-wet and her rain-soaked blond hair clinging like a seal's fur to her head and shoulders. One hand covered her mouth, as though to stifle a cry that was half-born there, and in her eyes were a great pleading and a great prayer as she watched her husband. But the cry did not find life. She uttered no sound. While she did not want Pieter to go, at the same time she knew that he must. Only if help came did anyone left alive on the *Spray* have even a faint chance of staying alive.

Then they were in the lake, and a mighty wave burst like a water-filled bomb about them. It staggered Ramsay and sent him reeling, but it did not unnerve him. Because he had practised in his own imagination what he must do from here on in, he could do it.

He felt cold water creeping about his shoes and then up around his knees. The boat which they had been dragging steadied itself as they reached water in which it could float. Through the blinding spray that lashed at them Ramsay looked across at Pieter. He saw him only indistinctly, but it was as though they read each other's thoughts. At exactly the same moment they flung themselves into opposite sides of the rower's seat and each grabbed an oar. The boy bent his back to the man-killing job of rowing.

The boat was sluggish, and again half-filled with water. But it floated, and as soon as they were free of the mighty waves that smashed against the beach it floated a little more easily. Ramsay looked back across the steel-gray turmoil to see the Van Hooven farm, and Marta still on the shore. Then he returned all his attention to the task at hand.

The lake was an insane thing, bent on destruction. They went into the trough of a wave and rose on the next one. Ramsay risked a fleeting backward glance to see the *Spray*, much nearer the shore and still afloat.

Suddenly they were in an almost-calm stretch of water. Ramsay felt cold fear run up and down his spine. He had met this on the sinking *Holter*, and now here it was again. Almost fearfully he glanced sidewise at Pieter, but he could not speak because the screaming wind would have drowned his words as soon as he uttered them. His eyes grew big.

Just behind, and again on the right side, an apparition drifted out of the depths. It was a ghost figure, a thing born of nightmares. Ramsay gasped. The White Sturgeon nosed to the surface, drifted lazily for a moment and disappeared back into the watery depths out of which it had come.

Ramsay risked a sidewise glance at Pieter, whose face remained undisturbed, and he swallowed the lump in his own throat. Sailors might fear the White Sturgeon, but if Pieter did, he was not showing his fear. The boy told himself again that the sturgeon was a fish, nothing more or less than a great fish which, through some freak of nature, was colored white. But it did seem to appear only when death and destruction stalked the lake. He forced such thoughts from his mind.

They were again in storm-lashed water, striving to keep their boat straight and headed toward the *Spray*. Vast waves bore down upon them, plunging the little craft into their cold troughs and then shooting it up as though it were a plaything. From the crest of the waves Ramsay could still see the *Spray*. He worried. Now there seemed to be only one man aboard her.

There was a sharp, sickening crack and the sound of splintering wood, that rose above the roar of the wind and the surge of the waves. The boat slewed sideways, and for the first time Pieter Van Hooven's face betrayed emotion. He brought in the stump of oar remaining in his hand and, at the risk of upsetting the little boat, leaned across the seat to snatch Ramsay's oar from its lock. With that in his hand, he made a precarious way to the stern. He thrust the oar over the rear seat, trying to use it as a rudder, and the boy strove to overcome the fear he felt.

The White Sturgeon, the sailors' superstition said, always brought disaster. If you see it, the little deck hand had told Ramsay, you can start praying right afterwards. For one terror-filled moment their predictions seemed correct. Twice Ramsay had seen the White Sturgeon; each time he had been in immediate danger of death. Then superstition subsided and reason came back to his aid.

Crouching in the back seat, with only one oar, Pieter Van Hooven was doing his best to fight the angry lake. Though he was a farmer, obviously he knew something of seamanship.

For a brief moment, just long enough to keep from capsizing, he kept the little boat headed into the onrushing waves. When he turned it, he did so skilfully. Working the oar only with the strength in his hard-muscled arms, he headed back towards shore. A mighty wave smashed the stern, throwing cold water over them and across the tiny craft. Ramsay moved from side to side, doing all he could to help Pieter by shifting his weight to where it was needed most. The boat was three-quarters filled with water. Never made for a heavy sea, now it was an almost dead thing. But so strong were the waves and so powerful the wind, that they were driven at almost motor speed back into the beach. Ramsay had one glimpse of Marta.

Pieter lost the little control he had. Turning sidewise, the boat lifted like a matchstick on the crest of a giant wave and spun dizzily down into the trough. It was lifted again, and just before it turned over Ramsay flung himself clear. As he did, he saw Pieter go over with him.

He dived as deeply as he could, knowing that the boat would come crashing down and knowing also that it would kill him if it struck him on the head. Far into the lake he went, swimming under water and groping his way. He surfaced to see the craft to one side and a bobbing object, which he thought was the head of Pieter Van Hooven. A second later a tremendous wave deposited him on the sandy beach.

He lay gasping, all the breath knocked out of him, and he wished desperately to get out of the path of the waves that were breaking over him. But it seemed impossible to move. His mind urged him to go, but he lacked the physical strength to obey. Then he felt a pair of hands in his armpits, and his body was dragged over the scraping sand. Ramsay looked up to see the frightened face of Marta Van Hooven.

"Can you move?" she pleaded.

"Gi—give me a minute!"

For what seemed an interminable time, but could not have been more than twenty seconds, Ramsay lay still. He turned over so that he lay face down, and lifted himself with his arms. His legs and feet were made of jelly. Vaguely he was aware of Marta and Pieter Van Hooven, one on each side, lifting him to his feet. A second later his strength returned.

Keening in from the lake, the wind made him stagger backwards. Reaching mountainous heights, the breaking waves shattered themselves far up on the beach. Ramsay looked across them. About two hundred yards out, the *Spray* was completely crippled. Trailing from her broken mast, the sail bled water into the angry lake. Down at the bows, the fisherman's boat seemed hung up on a rock or reef. Every second wave that washed in broke completely over her and hid her from view. But the single man remaining on board still worked calmly with the broken half of an oar, to free the *Spray* from her prison.

Ramsay allowed himself another split second. The entire dream was coming true. There were some men who, to the last, could meet the challenge of the lake with grace and spirit. The man on the *Spray*, identified even at this distance as Hans Van Doorst, had not given up.

The boy whirled on Pieter Van Hooven. "A coil of rope!" he ejaculated.

Without waiting to see whether or not Pieter followed his instructions, he raced for the barn. Snatching a bridle from its wooden peg, he went more slowly toward the corral where the little black horse was confined.

This had happened once before and it might happen again. A man's strength was as nothing in the raging lake, but a horse was many times as strong as a man. The black horse had brought him safely in when all the others had drowned.

The little horse arched his neck and flicked his ears when his young friend approached and patted him.

"Easy," Ramsay said reassuringly. "Take it easy, Black."

The little horse rested his head over the boy's shoulder for a moment, then the latter stepped back to slip the bit into Black's mouth, put the bridle over his ears and buckle the throat latch. The horse followed willingly behind him as he pushed the corral's gate aside.

He mounted, and Black reared and pranced, just to prove that he could. Ramsay tried not to look at the lake, but he couldn't help looking. When he did, very lonely in the gray waves, he saw the reef- or rock-bound *Spray*. The lone fisherman still could be seen, working to free his craft.

Ramsay leaned forward to pat the little horse on the neck. "We can do it," he murmured. "Let's prove it."

He took the bridle reins in his hand and trotted Black toward the foaming lake. Pieter, his eyes grave, tossed him a coil of half-inch rope. Ramsay had one glimpse of Marta's anguished face. He slipped the coil of rope over his shoulder and did not look back.

As they approached the lake, the horse hesitated, to paw the sand with a front hoof. He looked around to eye the rider on his back, and again Ramsay leaned forward. "All right," he said. "Go on."

The horse accepted his words but, more than that, his confidence. Guided by the bridle's touch, he walked willingly into the pounding lake. Another water bomb exploded about them. They submerged, but Black came up swimming strongly. Ramsay kept soft fingers on the bridle reins, not wanting to exert any pressure or do anything else that might divert the horse from the job at hand.

Tossing his head, Black sneezed to empty his nose of water that had washed into it. He was timing himself capably and almost perfectly to meet the waves at their place of least resistance, and he rose and fell with them. From the crests Ramsay could see the *Spray*. From the troughs he could see nothing. A lump rose in his throat.

The *Spray* was indeed sadly wounded. Only part of her stern showed above water. Hans Van Doorst still worked with a broken oar to free his boat, and as soon as he came near enough Ramsay knew that he had been right.

The Dutch fisherman had been one with the lake when Ramsay first saw him, and he was one with it now. Unafraid, he fought the lake as gracefully as a swordsman. Perched on the broken stump of mast, the sea gull fluttered his wings and clicked his mandibles.

Ramsay gauged the situation as precisely as he could. If he could throw his rope over the stranded *Spray*, the little horse might be able to pull it from its anchor and back to shore. Ramsay saw Hans Van Doorst turn to watch him. The fisherman waved a friendly hand.

Still guiding Black lightly, imposing no undue strain on the reins or bit, Ramsay steered him across the *Spray's* sunken prow. He let the reins hang slackly on the horse's neck and took the coil of rope from his shoulder. As precisely as he could, he cast and watched the rope snake through the air.

A sick feeling arose in the pit of his stomach and he moaned audibly. He had calculated the distance correctly but he had not allowed for the strength of the wind. The rope missed Hans Van Doorst's outstretched hands by two feet and fell into the angry lake. Of his own volition, Black turned back toward shore. Ramsay saw the squawking sea gull bounce a couple of feet into the air and spread his long wings. Grasping the reins, for the first time the boy used strength as he strove to turn the horse back. He glanced over his shoulder to see what might be done next, and gasped.

Hans Van Doorst had gone to the raised stern of his wrecked boat to give himself a running start, and as Ramsay looked, he dived. Leaping as far as possible from the *Spray* to avoid striking the rock, he hurled himself into the storm-lashed lake, straight at his would-be rescuers. For a few seconds that seemed like hours, he disappeared into the churning depths, but when he surfaced he was squarely behind Ramsay and he used both hands to grasp the horse's tail.

Black turned back toward shore. He swam more strongly now because he was going with the wind instead of against it, and his double burden did not seem unduly heavy. Ramsay saw Pieter and Marta Van Hooven, Pieter's hand protectingly over his wife's shoulder, as they waited to see what would happen.

The last wave burst around them and they were back on shore. Instantly Ramsay slid from the little horse's back and looked around. A nausea seized him. Hans Van Doorst was no longer in sight. Ramsay had tried and failed. He glanced toward the *Spray*, as though he expected to see the crazy Dutch fisherman still there, and knew only that waves were smashing the boat into kindling wood.

Then, as though he had literally risen from the lake, Hans Van Doorst picked himself up from the wreckage of a breaking wave and walked ashore. His tame sea gull fluttered out of the sky to alight on its master's shoulder. The Dutchman reached up to stroke his pet as he looked at Pieter and Ramsay. "None but me and Captain Klaus?" he asked.

"None, Hans," Pieter said.

For a moment an infinite sadness, a melancholy born thousands of years ago in the first fisherman who had seen his mates lost, pervaded the Dutchman. But it was only for a moment. Pieter and Ramsay walked to his side and offered their assistance. He declined it.

"I'll walk," he said.

Ramsay felt a great warmth for and a vast sympathy with this man who, while daring all and losing all, could remain so very human. Marta hovered solicitously near as they all went up to the house and wore their dripping clothes into her immaculate kitchen. Hans Van Doorst sat down, tried to fold his arms across his chest, and winced.

"You're hurt!" Marta cried.

"It is nothing." The Dutch fisherman looked at the three. "It happened out on the lake. We struck something, I do not know what. Perhaps the half-submerged hull of a sunken ship. Then we were in trouble."

Marta was stooping beside him, gently unbuttoning his soaking-wet shirt. Hans Van Doorst looked fondly down at her wet and bedraggled hair, and he offered no protest as his upper body was bared. There was a vast, ugly scar on the right side of his chest, and when Marta touched him there his ribs moved. The Dutchman sat very straight in his chair. Though he must have felt pain, he showed none.

Ramsay and Pieter stood aside while Marta worked expertly. Ripping one of her snow-white sheets into strips, she wound a bandage tightly around Hans Van Doorst's broken ribs. Ramsay and Pieter looked significantly at each other. Such an injury *might* have resulted when wind or a heavy wave flung the fisherman against something. Probably it had happened when Hans flung himself forward in an effort to rescue a shipmate.

Marta finished her bandaging and stepped back. "You rest now."

He grinned at her. "Fishermen have no time for rest."

"Do as she says, Hans," Pieter urged.

"Come," said Marta. She went to a bedroom, opened the door and waited expectantly.

Hans Van Doorst spread eloquent hands. "Who can argue with a woman?" he asked. "Especially a Dutch woman?"

He rose, went into the room, and closed the door behind him. Ten minutes later, Marta opened the door a crack and peeked in. She entered, and came out with Hans Van Doorst's clothing.

"He sleeps," she announced. "Like a man worn out he sleeps."

Ramsay changed his wet clothes for some dry ones Pieter had given him and went out to catch Black. From the house's ridge pole, Captain Klaus, Hans Van Doorst's tame sea gull, squawked at him. Ramsay grinned back, walked up to the little horse, rubbed him down, and put him back in the corral. He did the rest of his chores, and when he went into the house for dinner Hans Van Doorst was seated at the table.

"I told him!" Marta scolded. "I told him to stay in bed and I would bring him his food. But can I talk reason to a Dutchman?"

"Marta," Hans Van Doorst said softly, "there is fishing to be done."

Eager interest glowed in Pieter's eyes. "Are you going again, Hans?"

"I am a fisherman."

"You are crazy," Marta corrected. "One day you will kill yourself on that lake."

Again the sadness, the inborn melancholy, sat like a mask on the Dutch fisherman. But only for a moment.

"Marta," he said, "fishermen do not die in bed."

CHAPTER SIX

NEW VENTURE

Ramsay stirred sleepily and raised a restless hand to shield his eyes from the morning sun. Almost the whole night through, until the first waking birds had begun to chatter just outside his window, he had lain restlessly awake. Just thinking of Hans Van Doorst, and fishing, had not permitted him to sleep.

Now, with the sun high, he was at last deep in slumber. Ramsay could not know that Pieter had arisen shortly after the first birds and had the milking all finished, or that Hans Van Doorst sat in the kitchen, eating the hearty breakfast which Marta had prepared for him. He knew only that he seemed to be hearing strange sounds.

There were throaty chucklings and gurglings and low-pitched laughter, and all of it was punctuated by raucous squawks. Troubled, Ramsay rolled over in bed and covered his head with the quilt. Even that did not shut out the sounds, and finally he came fully awake. Sleepy-eyed, tousle-haired, he sat up in bed.

For a moment he could not define the sounds, which seemed to originate very near the roof of the house, and he was puzzled. Then he identified the various noises a sea gull makes. Ramsay slipped out of bed, pushed the double windows open, and looked into a calm morning.

There was a rustle of wings overhead and a flutter of feathers. Captain Klaus took strong wing to circle the house. He swung back to alight on the window ledge, and tilted his head sidewise while he regarded Ramsay with bright, intelligent eyes. "*Qu-uark!*" he chattered.

Ramsay grinned, but when he put out a hand to touch him Captain Klaus again took flight and sailed down to the now-calm lake. He alighted on the shore, folded his wings across his back, and walked down the beach until he found a storm-killed perch. With the fish in his bill, he flew back to the house's ridge-pole to eat his breakfast while he awaited the reappearance of Hans Van Doorst.

A little bit embarrassed, Ramsay dressed hurriedly. The working day in this country began with dawn and ended with dark. Everything that needed doing—and there was much to be done—had to be crowded into such daylight as there was, and there was never enough. Hurrying down the steps leading to the kitchen, he saw Hans Van Doorst at the table. Marta greeted him pleasantly, "Good morning."

"Good morning," Ramsay replied. "I overslept! I didn't mean to. Why didn't somebody call me?"

"Yaah!" Marta laughed. "Pieter said not to. You earned your sleep, Pieter said. Sit down with Hans and have some breakfast."

Hans said, "Men who are not hungry are sick. Sit down."

Ramsay sat, and felt a free and easy sense of comradeship, as though he and the Dutch fisherman had something in common. They felt alike and thought alike. Hans Van Doorst had thanked Ramsay with his eyes for rescuing him, but not once had he spoken of it and not once had he mentioned the wreck of the *Spray*. The boy was grateful for that; he knew that he would be embarrassed if his part in yesterday's incident were brought into the limelight.

Marta busied herself at the big wood-burning stove, and Ramsay speculated on the difficulties involved in just getting such a stove into this country. Marta laughed. "While I make you the breakfast, you listen to the crazy tales the crazy fisherman tells you."

Hans turned his twinkling eyes on Ramsay. "Marta is a good girl," he said. "A good Dutch girl. She thinks all men are crazy."

"They all are," Marta said. "Especially you. What you need is a good farm and stay away from that wild lake."

"Farms and me wouldn't get along, Marta." Hans laughed. "I told you I'm a fisherman."

"Yaah? You lost everything with the *Spray*. How are you going to go fishing again?"

Hans spread his two powerful hands. "These are what I had when I started. These are what I have now."

"You need money, too. Money for nets, money for ..."

The door opened and Pieter came in for breakfast. Hanging his light jacket on a wooden peg in the hallway, he took his seat at the table. "Why does Hans need so much money?" he asked.

"He says he's going fishing again." Marta sniffed. "I've been telling him that he should get a farm, and we can put him up until he gets one, and ..."

"Are you really going fishing?" Pieter broke in.

"That I am. I'm a fisherman. Now look, Pieter, you get up at dawn to milk your cows. No? To be sure, you get all the milk you can drink; but if you're lucky, Tradin' Jack Hammersly gives you maybe half of what your butter's worth. All winter long and all summer long you work for those cows. A fisherman, now, he works for four months, just four. . . ."

Pieter said, "It sounds good!"

"Pieter!" Marta broke in sharply. "You are *not* going fishing!"

Pieter wriggled uncomfortably. "Well," he said, "I can at least listen to what the man says, can't I?"

"One haul of the nets," Hans continued, "and maybe one thousand, maybe two thousand pounds of whitefish. Never less than five hundred. For that you get six cents a pound in the Chicago market. You don't earn that on your farm, and besides, fishing is a lot more fun. A smart Dutchman don't have to tend cows."

"*Uaah!*" Pieter breathed.

"Pieter!" Marta said.

Ramsay listened, dazzled by the prospects of a fisherman's life as compared to any future a farmer might have. Determinedly Marta brought a huge dish of wheat cakes and sausage over and thumped it firmly down on the table.

"Eat!" she commanded.

The three gave all their attention to the food, and they did not speak while eating. Then Hans pushed his chair back.

"If I am going to fish again, I must start," he announced. "First I will go down and see if there is any salvage."

"We'll help you!" Pieter exclaimed. "My boat was not badly smashed. A little work and it will be good as new."

"Pieter!" Marta said. "You are not going fishing!"

"Now I ask you," Pieter said plaintively, "is helping a man pick up his own property, his very own property, is that fishing? Could anyone even think it was fishing? No. Come on."

The three left the kitchen and walked down to the lake. Calm after the storm that had raged across it, only little waves were washing in. Ramsay looked out at the rock, as though half expecting to see the *Spray* still there, and saw nothing. Pieter gave a triumphant little exclamation and waded into shallow water to pick up something that bobbed back and forth.

It was the carved Valkyrie maiden that had been the *Spray's* figurehead. Exquisitely and almost perfectly hand-carved, the wooden statue leaned forward, as though she would embrace the whole lake to her bosom.

Hans Van Doorst's eyes were soft as he took it from Pieter. "My sweetheart!" he murmured.

Captain Klaus winged down from the ridge pole of the house to alight near them. Clucking softly to himself, happy because Hans was once more with him, he followed the three men down the beach. Ramsay found a coil of rope, then another, and farther on was the *Spray's* torn sail. Ramsay pointed out onto the lake.

"About there is where we saw the White Sturgeon," he said.

"I know," Hans Van Doorst murmured. "We saw him a half-dozen times."

Ramsay looked at him, puzzled. Then, "The sailors told me he always brings bad luck."

"The sailors!" Hans scoffed. "They know nothing about anything except maybe how to stuff themselves with good whitefish that the fishermen bring them! The White Sturgeon noses his way to the top when a storm comes, so he is bad luck? Do not believe it! He is good luck! He comes to the top so that he may show fishermen the way back to shore!"

Ramsay grinned appreciatively. This, in spite of the fact that the Dutch fisherman's idea of the White Sturgeon bringing good luck was as superstitious as the sailors' notion that he always brought bad, fitted in. It was what Hans should have said.

"How big is that sturgeon?" Ramsay asked.

"The Grandfather of all lake fish," Hans Van Doorst asserted solemnly. "Have you not noticed that, like all grandfathers, he is white? In truth, I have never seen a bigger fish anywhere."

"Another coil of rope!" Pieter said, pouncing on it.

Hans, who had grinned happily with each new find, did not even look around. Ramsay looked at him questioningly. Anything but stolid, the Dutch fisherman had been bubbling over at the prospect of going fishing again. Now he seemed melancholy, immersed within himself, and his whole attention was given to the lake.

Ramsay followed his gaze, but saw little. True, a vast number of small aquatic worms had been washed ashore by the pounding waves. There must have been countless millions of them, so many that they formed a living carpet as far up the beach as the waves had washed. The wriggling, writing mass was now disentangling itself, and the worms that could were crawling back into the lake. A number of sea gulls and a number of land birds were gorging themselves, and new birds arrived by the flock. They scarcely made a dent in the multitude of worms. Ramsay looked again at Hans Van Doorst.

"Never, never!" the fisherman breathed.

Pieter, too, swung to look curiously at him. "What's the matter, Hans?"

"I went on the lake when I was a boy of thirteen," Hans Van Doorst said. "That was fourteen years ago, in 1852. I thought I had seen much, but never have I seen this!"

"What?" Ramsay asked impatiently.

"Look around you," Hans said. "What do you see?"

"Worms."

"Not worms! Food for whitefish! With these millions washed up, can you not imagine the vast amount remaining in the water? We are all rich men!"

"You think so?" Pieter queried.

"There is no doubt of it! The whitefish go where their food is! There must be countless tons of whitefish here at your very door step, and here is where we shall fish!"

"Do whitefish eat only worms?" Ramsay asked.

"No. They feed on other things, too, notably their own spawn or that of other fish. But enough of this idle talk! I must have a net so we can start fishing at once! Pieter, I would borrow your horse and cart!"

"The cart you may have," Pieter said. "The horse belongs to Ramsay."

"Go ahead and take him," Ramsay urged.

Hans tripped like a dancer to the barn, caught the little horse, and backed him between the shafts of Pieter's two-wheeled cart. Bubbling like a boiling kettle, entirely happy, he started at a fast trot up the sand beach to Three Points. With a startled squawk, Captain Klaus hurried to catch up. The tame sea gull settled affectionately on the rim of the cart's seat.

As Ramsay watched him go, he felt a vast envy of the light-hearted fisherman. If ever he could go away like that, he thought, he would have lived life at its fullest. Not until he looked around did he discover that Pieter was watching too, and his eyes were wistful.

"There is work to be done!" Marta called.

They flushed and walked towards the barnyard, where Marta was tending her poultry. Geese, chickens and ducks swarmed around her and pigeons alighted on her shoulders. She kept her eyes on the men.

As Ramsay and Pieter cleaned the cowbarn, both remained strangely silent. Both thought of the Dutch fisherman. Then Pieter, who had promised to have a dressed pig ready for Tradin' Jack Hammersly, started honing a razor edge on his butchering tools. Ramsay picked up a hoe, preparatory to returning to the corn-patch.

"You think he'll get a net?" Pieter asked.

"I hope so!"

Moodily, scarcely seeing or knowing what he was doing, Ramsay chopped at weeds that had stolen a home in the growing corn. The work suddenly lacked any flavor whatever. Millions of worms, whitefish food, washed up on the beach and the bay in front of Pieter's swarming with whitefish! That's what the Dutch fisherman had said. Marta brought his mid-morning lunch, and her eyes were troubled.

"Do you think Hans will get what he wants?" she asked.

"I don't know. Marta, why don't you want Pieter to go fishing?"

"You heard what he said. Last night he said it. Fishermen do not die in bed. Those were his words."

"Just talk. The lake's safe enough."

"Yaah? Is that why Joe Mannis can make more money than anybody else around here, just watchin' bodies? Aah! I worry about my man!"

Ramsay said gently, "Don't worry, Marta."

Marta returned to the house and Ramsay continued working. In back of the barn Pieter had his butchered pig strung up on a block and tackle, and the two men looked at each other. Both were waiting for Hans Van Doorst to return.

About a half-hour before noon Captain Klaus soared back to his accustomed place on the house's ridge pole. A moment later the little black horse appeared on the beach, and Hans drove to the barn.

Ramsay and Pieter, meeting him, stifled their astonishment. When Hans left them, to all outward appearances he had been a normal person. Now blood had dried on his nose and his right eye was puffy and streaked with color. Anger seethed within him.

"There is no honor any more!" he said bitterly. "And men are not men!"

"What happened?" Ramsay inquired.

"What happened? I went to Three Points to get us a pound net! Carefully did I explain to that frog-mouthed Fontan, whose wife knits the best pound nets on Lake Michigan, what I wanted. I know pound nets cost five hundred dollars, but I was very careful to prove that we have untold riches just waiting to be caught! As soon as we made some catches, I said, we would pay him his money, plus a bonus for his trouble. Fontan became abusive."

"Then what?" Pieter said.

"He hit me twice. Because of these thrice-cursed broken ribs I cannot move as swiftly as I should. Then I hit him once, and the last I saw of him he was lying on one of his wife's pound nets. After that came the constable who, as everybody knows, is merely another one of Devil Chad's playthings, and said he would put me in jail. It was necessary to hit the constable, too."

Hans Van Doorst leaned against the side of the barn, glumly lost in his own bitter thoughts. Coming from the house to meet Hans and sensing the men's moodiness, Marta fell silent beside her husband. Ramsay unhitched the little black horse, put him back into the corral, and hung the harness on its wooden pegs.

After five minutes, Pieter Van Hooven broke the thick silence. "I do not know whether or not it will be any good, perhaps not. But last year a fisherman came here in a very small boat. He was going to Three Points, he said, to get himself a larger boat and he had to make time. I do not know what happened to him, for he never came back and I have not seen him since. Probably Joe Mannis got him. But before he took his leave he asked me to store for him a box of nets and ..."

"A box of nets!" Hans Van Doorst's melancholy left him like a wind-blown puff of feathers. He put an almost passionate arm about Pieter's shoulders. "All is lost! All is gone! Then this—this miracle worker! He talks of a box of nets! Tell me, Pieter! Tell me it is still there!"

"It must be, for it was never taken away," Pieter said.

"Then let us get it! Let us get and look at it before I faint with excitement!"

Pieter and Hans disappeared in the barn, and a moment later they reappeared with a long, deep wooden box between them. Having lain in the barn for a year, the box and its contents were thick with dust and spiders had woven their own gossamer nets everywhere. Hans Van Doorst patted the dust away. He looked with ecstatic eyes, and he unfolded a few feet of the net. Ramsay saw that it was similar to the gill net insofar as it had stones—sinkers—on one side and a place for floats on the other. Made of sixteen-thread twine, the net had a three-inch mesh.

"A seine," Hans Van Doorst pronounced, "and a well-made seine, though it was not made in Two Rivers. It was brought here by one of the Ohio fishermen, for that is the way they tie their meshes. Let us see some more. I would say that it is about eight hundred feet long. That is not ample; we still need good pound nets, but with it we may again go fishing. Help me, Pieter."

Pieter and Hans dragged the box to a small tree, tied one end of the seine to the tree's trunk, and began to unwind the net toward another little tree. Ramsay saw how shrewdly the Dutch fisherman had guessed. The trees, within a few feet one way or the other, were just about eight hundred feet apart and Hans Van Doorst tied the other end of the seine to the far tree. He stood still, a small happy grin lighting his face, and looked at their discovery.

Slowly, with Ramsay, Marta and Pieter trailing him, he started to walk the length of the seine as it lay on the ground. He kept his eyes downward, and as he walked along he talked almost to himself. "A good seine, yes, a good seine, but it has received hard use. Here is almost five feet where it scraped among sharp rocks, and the mesh is worn. Under a heavy load of fish, it will break. That hole was made by a sunken log or other object, for you can see that it is a clean tear. This one was made by a huge fish, probably a sturgeon, for just see how the mesh is mangled where he lunged time after time against it. Now this . . ."

Slowly, missing no inch of the seine, he traveled the length of it, and as he traveled he marked every hole and weak spot by telling himself about it. Reaching the end, he stood nervously tapping a finger against his forehead. "My hands are more accustomed to pulling seines than mending them," he told the three. "Still, if we are to make the catch we can make, this seine must be mended. I will try to mend it."

"I worked on a net in Three Points!" Ramsay said eagerly. "I stayed for a while with Pierre LeDou, and because there was nothing else to kill time, I helped Madame LeDou knit a gill net! This cannot be too different!"

"You!" For a moment Ramsay thought Hans was going to kiss him. "So! Everything works our way! Yaah? You fix the seine!" His face fell. "No. We must have new twine. Now where will I get it?"

"I have some," Marta spoke up. "Good linen twine, easily a match for anything in this seine."

"And you would give it?" Pieter asked incredulously.

Marta shrugged. "You're going fishing, anyway, and I'm going with you. Men always want all the fun."

The smile Hans turned on her was rare. "A good Dutch girl," he said. "Thank you, Marta."

Pieter and Hans cut tripods—three poles strung together at the top to form a standard—and at necessary intervals raised the seine to them so that it was completely off the ground. Like a huge tennis net, broken only by the tripods, it stretched between the two trees. Ramsay stood beside it with a one and one-half inch meshboard—this mesh was three inches—and a ball of the fine linen twine which Marta had given him.

He worked as fast as he could, while at the same time he did not sacrifice efficiency. More than ever fishing seemed to be an art within itself, and if the seine were not perfectly made, then it was better left alone. A slipshod or hasty knot could cost them a hundred pounds of fish, or even the seine itself. As Ramsay went along, he judged for himself which parts needed repairing. Any mesh that seemed to be worn must be replaced; a whole school of fish might follow each other through a single hole.

For half an hour Hans stood watching him. Then, satisfied that Ramsay knew what he was about, he went off to cut new floats and place them on top of the seine. A dozen times he went down to study the bay, looking carefully and judging for himself the depth at which they would find the largest schools of whitefish. Coming back, he adjusted the stone sinkers accordingly.

Absorbed in his work, Ramsay gave no thought to the passage of time until Marta called him for supper. As soon as he had finished eating, he returned to the net. Darkness deepened and still he worked on.

"Ach!" Marta said. "You'll kill yourself working! Can you not come in now?"

"Just a little while. Bring me a lantern."

Ramsay heard Hans Van Doorst murmur, "A fisherman, that one," and a yellow lantern glowed behind him. It was nothing more than a tallow candle set in a glass case but, Ramsay thought, he really didn't need a stronger light. So sensitive had his fingers become to the feel of the net, and so expert was he in knitting new meshes, that, almost, he would have been able to do it with his eyes closed. He worked on while, held alternately by Hans and Pieter, the lantern moved with him. He forgot the ache in his fingers and the weariness in his body. He knew only that the sooner the net was in good working order, the sooner they could go fishing.

The pre-dawn birds were again singing when Ramsay finally bumped against something and, so absorbed had he been in his work, it took him a moment to realize that it was the other tree. He held the mesh board in fingers which, strangely and suddenly, seemed to lack all nerve or feeling. He blinked almost stupidly and stepped back.

When he spoke, his words sounded almost silly. "Well," he said, "there it is."

"There indeed it is!" Hans chuckled. "And there it will be until, as soon as possible, we get it into the water. Come now and sleep, for with the morning's sun I would have you go with me."

Ramsay stumbled to his bedroom, took his shoes off, and without removing any of his other clothing, fell across the bed. Instantly he was submerged in exhausted slumber from which he was awakened by a gentle hand on his shoulder.

"Come now," a voice said.

Ramsay sat up with a start, to see Hans Van Doorst looking down at him. Again with a guilty feeling, he knew that he had slept far beyond the time when any worker in this country should sleep. Hastily he sprang out of bed. "I'll be right with you!"

"Compose yourself," said Hans Van Doorst, who had awakened him. "There is no need for any mad rush. I thought you might wish to help me."

"Oh, sure!"

Ramsay grinned faintly when he discovered that, except for his shoes, he was fully dressed. He put his shoes on and tied them, went outside to wash at the wash stand, and came in to eat the breakfast Marta had ready. Scarcely noticing what he ate, he gulped it down.

"Easy," Marta cautioned. "The stomach complaint you will be giving yourself!"

"I must hurry! Hans is waiting for me!"

"With men it is always hurry, especially when they go to do what they wish to do anyway. Aah! Only a man would give up a good farm to go fishing!"

"Pieter has not given up his farm," Ramsay pointed out.

"He will," Marta prophesied. "He will, and he will go fishing with you and that crazy Hans."

"Oh, Marta, don't be so sad about things! It ..."

She was sunny again. "Go along now. Hans is waiting."

Hans had Black hitched to the cart and was waiting outside the door. His wings calmly folded, Captain Klaus sat on the back of the seat. Ramsay climbed up, and Hans slapped the reins over the horse's back. They started up the sand beach—there was a corduroy road but the sand was smoother—toward Three Points.

Ramsay grinned impishly as they drove through the town, because he felt the questioning glances of the towns people. Devil Chad controlled all this, and Devil Chad had made it very clear that Ramsay was not wanted in Three Points. Maybe Hans wasn't wanted either but, as Pierre LeDou had pointed out, the fishermen and farmers cared little what anyone else thought. Ramsay looked about, hoping to see Devil Chad, but he was nowhere in sight. A little disappointed, he relaxed beside Hans.

They drove through the village and up a rutted little road that wound among gloomy hemlocks. Ramsay saw a doe with a fawn at her side, staring at them. As they drew near the doe raised her white tail over her back and disappeared. Hans grinned at her.

"They shoot the mammas with the babies," he said, "just like they do the papas with the horns. There is no more right in that than there is in netting a spawning fish."

"You mean because the babies will die?"

"Yaah. Then, after there aren't any more deer, people just do not understand it. Some awful disease, they say, carried them off. They do not know that their own lack of sense carried them off. It is the same with fish. Those who seine in the spawning season kill maybe two hundred for every one they take. When there are not any more fish, they will invent a terrible disease that carried them off."

Ramsay felt a little alarm. "Do you think there won't be any more?"

"The whitefish," Hans pronounced, "cannot last in numbers such as you find them in now. That is because so many of them are being caught. For maybe ten thousand years they are filling the lake until now no fish is more numerous. Yaah, for many years they were a food staple of the Indians. I myself have seen Indians spearing them, or shooting them with bows and arrows. Tribes came from as far as the Mississippi River to fish here. But a net fisherman takes more in one season than a whole tribe of Indians used to, and often the fishermen cannot even take care of what they catch. I have seen whitefish, good eating whitefish, stacked like cordwood along the beach and left to rot there. I have seen them fed to pigs. The best fishing along Lake Erie is already gone, due to such excesses. That is why fishermen from Ohio come here."

"Will fishing end?" Ramsay inquired.

"That I do not think. Considering it from all angles. Now a fisherman will catch perhaps a thousand whitefish, and maybe a hundred sturgeon, for every trout. Why? Because the whitefish and sturgeon eat trout spawn is part of the reason. When the whitefish and sturgeon are gone, the trout will multiply until they are the big catch. If the trout are taken or die out, there will be something else. No. There will always be fishing here, but it will be better when men learn to fish wisely and not to take anything in the spawning season."

"When is that?" Ramsay inquired.

"Whitefish and trout both spawn in the fall, from the fifteenth of October until the fifteenth of December. The sturgeon, I think they are a river fish and that they go up the rivers to spawn. If ever the rivers are closed, there will be many fewer sturgeon."

The gloomy little road swerved back toward the lake. They broke out of the trees, and Ramsay saw the water again. Built into it, at this point, was a rambling wooden pier. There was a house and a fishing shanty. Tied to a stake in a patch of green grass, a sad-eyed brown cow munched placidly on a five-pound whitefish. Tied to the pier, a saucy twenty-six-foot Mackinaw boat, much like the *Spray*, bobbed up and down. Nearer the beach was another boat, evidently a sadly worn one. Nets of various kinds were strung on reels close to the lake.

The house's door opened, and a ferocious little black dog snarled toward them. Showing white teeth, foaming at the mouth, he hurled himself straight at the visitors. Hans laughed and swung down from the cart, and as soon as he did the little black dog leaped about him to wag an almost furious welcome. Hans grinned and knelt to tickle the dog's ears.

"Like most Frenchmen, you can do nothing unless you do it violently," he soothed. "Where is your master?"

The house's door opened and a man, whom at first Ramsay thought was a boy, flung himself out. Barely five feet tall, he was dressed in breeches, leather leggings with colored fringes and a shirt that seemed to sport every color in the rainbow. He threw himself at Hans.

"*Mon ami!*" he screamed. "My friend! It has been so long, so very long since you honored us with a visit! Tell me what has kept you away for so very long?"

"Baptiste," Hans said, "meet one of my new partners, Ramsay Cartou. Ramsay, Baptiste LeClaire."

Baptiste wrung Ramsay's arm as though it were a pump handle and in spite of his small size, he was very strong. He looked frankly at the boy.

"You have," he asked, "bought an interest in the *Spray*?"

"The *Spray* is no more," Hans informed him. "She went back to the lake."

"Oh."

For a moment Baptiste was very sober. Then both men laughed, as though they shared some huge secret which nobody else could ever understand. Baptiste exploded.

"What is it you need, my friend? My boats, my nets, my pier, my life? Name it and it is yours!"

"No," Hans said. "What we need is barrels. Good oaken barrels with pliant black ash hoops. We also need salt. We have a net and we have a boat."

"That is all you need?" Baptiste seemed disappointed.

"That is all."

Baptiste turned and in rapid-fire French directed orders at three men who were lingering near. At once they began to take barrels built to hold two hundred pounds of fish from a huge pile near the fishing shanty and to stack them on Baptiste's boat. Ramsay read her name, *Bon Homme*. Baptiste LeClaire turned to his visitors.

"Now that you are here," he said, "share the hospitality of my poor home."

"With pleasure," Hans agreed.

They went into the house to meet Baptiste's wife, a sparkling little black-eyed French woman. Producing the inevitable jug, Baptiste filled three gourds with fiery whisky. Hans and Baptiste drained theirs with one gulp. Ramsay nursed his, both men laughed at him. But the boy could partake of the delicious fish stew which Baptiste's wife prepared.

A half-hour after Ramsay and Hans returned to the Van Hooven farm, a white sail bloomed out in the bay. She was the *Bon Homme*, loaded halfway up the mast with barrels and salt. Hans Van Doorst rubbed his hands in undisguised glee.

"Now," he chuckled, "we go fishing!"

CHAPTER SEVEN

PARTNERS

Ramsay was puzzled. Hans Van Doorst had arisen even before the first faint streaks of dawn cracked the night sky and without waiting for anyone else to get up, or for breakfast, he had gone out to work. He was not fishing, for he had assured Ramsay that there would be no fishing until all could take part. Furthermore, Hans had said, the fishing would need all of them. One man alone could not take enough fish to make it worthwhile.

Still, Hans had gone out before it was properly light enough to see. Ramsay had heard Captain Klaus greet his master from the top of the house. What anyone would be doing out of bed at such an early hour remained a mystery. In the dim morning light, descending the steps to the kitchen, Ramsay continued to wonder why Hans had gone out when he did. He greeted the Van Hoovens, who were already washed up for breakfast, and Marta went to the back door to call, "Hans!"

Captain Klaus' hoarse squawk broke the morning stillness, and a second later there was an answering call from Hans. He was down at the beach, doing something there, and presently he came in.

Ramsay grinned appreciatively at his appearance, for the Dutch fisherman's cheeks glowed like the rising sun. His eyes sparkled, and a perpetual chuckle seemed to gurgle in his throat. Plainly Hans had been doing some invigorating work, but it was work in which he took a vast pleasure. Anything onerous could not possibly put such a shine upon anyone at all. Hans washed at the basin outside the door.

"Ah!" he breathed as he sat down to the huge breakfast Marta had readied. "This looks good!"

"I should think a stale crust would look good to anyone who puts in a half-day's work before anyone else stirs," Marta said.

"It would!" Hans agreed, helping himself to half a dozen eggs and an equal number of bacon slices. "It would, and many a time I have dined on only a crust! But fare such as this! Fit for the angels! I'm the luckiest fisherman alive, I think!"

"Also the most oily-tongued," Marta added. Nonetheless she was pleased. "I suppose, when we are all wealthy from fishing, you will hire a cook for me?"

"Not I!" Hans said. "Never I! Hiring anyone but you to do our cooking would be as out of place as hiring Joe Mannis instead of a preacher to do our praying! No, Marta! Not elsewhere in Wisconsin is there one who equals your skill with cookery!"

Pieter, who often tried to beguile his wife but seldom succeeded, laughed. Marta blushed. While Hans devoured what he had already taken, then served himself to three more eggs, Ramsay ate almost feverishly. Today was the big day, the time all of them had been waiting for, because today they went fishing. Ramsay finished and waited with ill-concealed impatience while Pieter and Hans mopped their plates with crusts of bread. All three went outside.

Squawking and chuckling, as though at some huge joke, Captain Klaus winged down from the rooftop to alight on his master's shoulder. He tilted, flapping his wings to balance himself, and caressed Hans' cheek with his hard, cold bill, even while he kept up a running fire of sea gull chatter. Hans reached up to stroke his pet.

Ramsay looked down at the beach, and saw two structures which had not been there yesterday. Hans must have built them this morning. They were windlasses, made of peeled logs, and about eight hundred feet apart. One was the conventional windlass—a drum mounted on two uprights and with a crank that could be turned by hand. The spindle of the other—all these lake men could work miracles with logs or anything else at their command—was set vertically in a stone and log foundation and it had a long, stout shaft protruding from its center. Ramsay looked questioningly at Hans.

The Dutch fisherman shrugged. "It is simple," he explained. "We have but one horse. Therefore, we men work the one while the horse turns the other. Marta can lead it."

Ramsay was incredulous. "You mean we'll take so many fish that a horse will be needed to drag them in?"

Hans' throaty chuckle sounded. "If we do not," he said, "from now on forever you may say that Hans Van Doorst is not a fisherman. Say that he is just a little boy who plays at fishing."

With a fisherman's skill, Hans was coiling a rope. He settled it carefully in the bottom of the boat, so that it wouldn't kink or snarl when paid out, and was alert to avoid stepping on or tangling it in anyway. Folded exactly as Hans wanted it, with all the floats on one side and all the sinkers on the other, the net was overhauled on the stern of the boat. Another coil of rope lay on the net, and Hans tied one end of that to the spindle of the horse-powered windlass.

Then he looked happily at Pieter and Ramsay. "Now," he said, "I need an oarsman."

"I'll row!" Ramsay offered eagerly.

"Go ahead." Pieter grinned.

So expertly that he scarcely ruffled the water and did not even disturb his net or rope, Hans launched the boat. He waded in up to his knees, paying out more rope as he did so, and held the boat steady until Ramsay waded out beside him and climbed into the rower's seat.

Ramsay tried to board cautiously, skilfully, as he had seen Hans do. Obviously a great deal of careful work had gone into folding the net and coiling the rope. Everything had to be done exactly right, and one clumsy or ill-timed move could make a hopeless snarl out of all. Still, Hans seemed confident and sure of himself. Probably, Ramsay thought, he had done this so many times that doing it was almost second nature. The boy looked expectantly at Hans.

"Straight into the lake," the Dutch fisherman directed. "Keep a straight right-angle course to the windlass; you can do that by sighting yourself from it. Row as swiftly as you wish."

With strong, surging strokes of the oars, Ramsay sent the ponderous boat out into the quiet lake. He watched Hans carefully, trying to note everything he did, and his respect for fishermen grew. The Dutchman sat almost carelessly in the stern, to all outward appearances not even interested in what he was doing. But, as they continued out into the lake, the rope continued to slip smoothly over the stern. There was never a tangle or even a kink. It looked easy, but net-weaving had looked easy too before Ramsay tried it. Beyond any doubt, it took skill and long familiarity with the job to handle six or eight hundred feet of rope in such a fashion and do it perfectly.

They came near the end of the rope and Ramsay slowed his strokes a little. The laughing Dutch fisherman turned to him.

"Sharp left," he directed. "Stay about this far out in the lake and row a bit more slowly. Now we set the seine."

Ramsay followed instructions, watching the beach line to make sure that he stayed the proper distance out, and Hans began sliding the seine over the stern. He did it smoothly, gracefully, as he did everything connected with fishing. Ramsay nodded approvingly to see how well Hans laid his net and how expertly he had guaged the place in which it was to be laid. Instead of curling toward the beach, the seine, obviously controlled by a current that swept into the lake, billowed outward.

"Does the lake have different currents?" Ramsay asked interestedly.

"That it does. When the wind blows toward shore, of course waves wash up on the shore. But the lake, she moves in a thousand different ways, and the currents that appear on the surface are not always like those that surge beneath the surface. Ah, yes! Many moods has Lake Michigan and," Hans grinned, "not many of them are placid moods."

"How could you tell that a current to hold the seine was right here?"

"I felt it when I had hold of your horse's tail."

Ramsay pondered that information. The current holding the net certainly was not perceptible from the surface. It would not be evident at all, except to one who had a thorough understanding of such things and was able to sense the most minute change in the water that lay about him. Of course, the stones, the sinkers, probably helped hold the seine in place too.

Foot by foot, the seine slipped into the lake and a long line of it stretched at an angle toward the boat. Ramsay tried to judge for himself how far the net was going down. He could not because he had had too little experience in fishing, but he was sure the seine rested exactly where Hans wanted it to rest.

Without seeming to move, Hans leaned over to pick up the other coil of rope. Smoothly he tied it, and the last few feet of seine slid over the boat's stern to disappear in the lake. Ramsay waited expectantly for directions. They came.

"Straight as you can towards the other windlass," Hans said. "Then we are all ready."

Again Ramsay turned at a right angle toward the other windlass. Now he began to understand the setting of a seine. There were the two windlasses, the two six-hundred-foot ropes and the seine running parallel to the beach. Now, Ramsay supposed, they would beach the boat, tie this rope to the other windlass, and be ready to haul in the seine. If they did not make a good catch, they could lengthen the ropes and put the seine farther out in the lake. Also, by adding more sinkers or subtracting some, they could raise or lower the seine. Ramsay tried to make some observations about the water in which they were fishing.

It was comparatively shallow, though at all places except very near the shore it would float a fair-sized ship. Also, it seemed to have a rather smooth bottom. In addition, though the bay could at times be angry, it was more sheltered than some places. Storms here probably would at no time reach the heights of fury that they reached on the open lake. Because he was anxious to learn as much as he could about fishing, Ramsay asked some questions. "Are whitefish usually found in shallow water?"

"Almost always," Hans said. "Though they need not necessarily always be found close to shore. I myself know of reefs where we will be sure of wonderful catches as soon as we get some pound nets, and some of them are a mile or more out."

"Then the lake bottom varies?"

"Oh, yes! To get an idea of what the bottom of the lake is like, take a look at the land about you. Here you find a hill, or a succession of rolling hills. Here is a stretch of flat prairie. There are deep gulches and bluffs. You will find clay, sand, loam, small stones, boulders. As I've already said, the lake's bottom is almost exactly like the land about it."

"What's the deepest part?"

"Baptiste LeClaire and I once sounded a place off the Wisconsin peninsula. We touched bottom with a thousand feet of line, and I think that may be the deepest place in Lake Michigan, though I cannot be sure. I have not sounded every place in the lake and, for that matter, neither has anyone else."

"Are there deep-water fish?"

"The trout ordinarily seeks deep water, though they may be found in shallows in the spring. However, there are not enough trout to be worth a fisherman's while. Some day this may change."

"Is there any way to set a net so a fisherman may be sure of a good catch?"

"Not once in ten times, if he is just beginning, can a fisherman be certain of a good catch, or of any catch. The tenth time is the exception. I am sure, for instance, that there must be a vast number of whitefish in this bay, because the food for them is here. Otherwise, the fisherman must be taught by experience, or by another fisherman, where to set his nets so that he will make a good catch. Watch it now. We are about to land."

The nose of the little boat bumped gently against the sand beach, and Hans stepped out into knee-deep water. Paying no attention to his soaking-wet shoes and trousers, he uncoiled the rope as he walked up the beach and tied it through a hole which he had drilled in the spindle of the hand windlass. More gingerly, not afraid of getting wet but not anxious to do so, Ramsay stepped to the nose of the boat and leaped onto the dry beach.

Pieter and Marta joined them, and all turned puzzled glances on Hans; they knew almost nothing about the technique of fishing and must look to him.

Ramsay watched the fisherman test the taut rope with his hand, and a little smile of satisfaction flitted across his face.

Excited himself, Hans looked at the even more excited people about him. "Relax." He grinned. "The seine is not going anywhere, and we will soon see what we have caught. Ramsay, do you want to harness the horse and bring him down?"

"Sure."

Ramsay trotted to the barn, anxious to be doing anything that would help relieve the seething tension within him. Everything he had done this morning—indeed, everything he had done since meeting Hans Van Doorst—had been fascination itself. Now, if Hans' predictions were right, and the Dutch fisherman seemed so absolutely sure of himself, they would soon be in the fishing business. Ramsay laid a friendly hand on Black's mane, and the little horse followed willingly into the barn. He stood quietly to be harnessed. Ramsay fastened a singletree to the harness tugs and hooked a strong chain onto it.

Partaking of the humans' excitement, Captain Klaus winged low over the beach, crying and squawking as he wheeled and dipped in graceful circles. Ramsay grinned at him. Of all the pets a fisherman might have, surely a sea gull was the most fitting.

Ramsay led Black toward the far windlass, the one the horse was to work, because Hans, Pieter and Marta had gathered about it. Captain Klaus came out of the sky to alight on top of the windlass, and the horse scraped a restless front hoof across the sand beach. Ramsay looked inquiringly at Hans, who frowned and stepped back, then turned to the boy. "We need a longer chain," he decided. "Will you get one?"

"Sure."

Ramsay ran back to the barn and returned with the longest chain Pieter had. Hans hooked it to the windlass shaft, laid it out flat, and then connected it to the chain Ramsay had already brought. The boy nodded understandingly. The rope dipped into the lake, then rose to the windlass spindle. The chain had to be long enough so that the horse, in walking around and around, could step over the rope.

Hans turned to Marta. "When I give the word," he said, "lead the horse in a circle around the windlass. Lead him slowly; we do not want the seine to come in too fast. Try to maintain a steady pace, and we will do our best to suit ours to yours. Both ends of the seine must come in evenly."

"Yaah!" In spite of her dire forebodings about fishermen, Marta's eyes were shining like stars. "Yaah! I can do it."

"Good," Hans said gently. "I know you can. Ramsay, you and Pieter come with me."

The three men took their places by the other windlass, and Ramsay tried to suppress a growing excitement. He waited tensely, both hands on the crank; Pieter was on the other side of the windlass.

Looking once more at the taut rope stretching into the lake, Hans Van Doorst raised his voice, "All right, Marta!"

Grasping the cheek strap of the little horse's bridle, Marta began to lead him slowly around and around. Tense, sweating a little, Ramsay took a fierce grip on the windlass crank and looked at Hans. The Dutch fisherman, his eyes on Marta, timed the turning of the windlass. "Now!" he said.

Ramsay strained with every muscle and nerve, and great beads of sweat dripped from his forehead. Hans had built well and with a full appreciation of leverage and tension; nevertheless, the windlass was hard to turn. The seine itself would be responsible for part of that. Dry, one man could carry it. But when lake water penetrated every one of its hundreds of meshes, the seine would surely weigh much more. However, no net of any description could within itself weigh this much. Hans must have guessed correctly. There were endless fish in the bay and the incoming seine must be loaded with them.

"Faster!" Hans exclaimed.

Ramsay gritted his teeth and turned the windlass faster. He shot a fleeting glance at Marta, who was still leading the horse slowly. Even so, Black was going too fast. The combined strength of three men was no match for the strength of a horse. Hans' bellow split the air, "Marta, stop!"

Marta halted the little horse and Ramsay leaned his weight against the windlass' crank so that they would not lose what they had already gained. He gulped in great, refreshing breaths. Hans asked, "Can you hold it?"

Ramsay and Pieter nodded, and Hans walked down to talk with Marta. She must lead the horse even more slowly, for the men could not keep up with him. If both ends of the seine were not pulled in evenly, if the net was tilted or bent, the catch could well be lost.

Ramsay straightened as Hans came back to take hold of the crank. "All right," he said.

Ramsay turned, setting his shoulder to the windlass while his breath came in excited little gasps. The rope, tight as a stretched wire, sloped into the lake. Though it was stoutly built of heavy logs, the windlass trembled on its frame. The crank became harder to turn and the wet rope wrapped like a clinging hair about the spindle. Ramsay gasped.

Out in the lake, just beyond the shallow water at the edge of the beach, the seine's floats showed. The seine itself was bent like a bow, its two ends straining toward the windlasses while the center arched into the lake.

The gleam of silver in the seine seemed to cast a soft radiance over the lake and the beach, and even a powerful current could not have bowed the seine in such a fashion. Ramsay set his shoulder to the windlass and helped give it two more turns. Down at the other windlass, Marta was watching them. She, too, had learned. The men could not keep up with the horse, so she was adjusting the horse's speed to them.

Farther up the seine came, so that some of the sinkers were dragging in the shallows. The floats were bowed over, forming a sort of half-sack, and the center of the seine still arched back into deep water. Ramsay saw a tight little grin appear on Hans Van Doorst's face. Pieter was looking incredulously at the loaded net.

"A little more!" Hans pleaded. "Just a little more! Get the center up!"

They took two more turns, brought the center of the seine into shallow water, and Hans latched the windlass. With a wild whoop, the Dutch fisherman raced down to the lake and stooped to grasp a hundred-and-fifty-pound sturgeon caught in the net. Hans dragged it up onto the beach, left it there, and returned to get a bigger one.

"Nets unload!" he sang out.

Ramsay ran forward, heedless of water that surged about his knees. He stumbled, fell headlong, and arose sputtering. But, now that he was soaking-wet anyway, it no longer made any difference. He grabbed a six-pound whitefish in each hand and threw the pair far up the beach. He grinned as he watched Pieter drag another big sturgeon out of the seine, and grabbed two more whitefish.

"Yaah! For once men work with a real will!"

Ramsay turned around to see Marta, her spray-wet hair plastered close to her head. Her feet were spread almost defiantly apart, and the smile on her lips and the laugh in her eyes were proof of the fact that she was now whole-heartedly with them. Fishermen risked a lot. But who didn't risk when they played for big stakes? Lake Michigan was there, until now an almost untapped source of wealth; and if nobody dared to get this hoard, it would remain forever in the lake. Somebody had to try. In that moment, as never before, Ramsay knew that they were in the fishing business.

Only vaguely was he aware of Pieter and Hans working beside him, and he did not know how long it took to get all the fish out of the seine. He knew only that suddenly the net sagged emptily. He took two small whitefish out of it, threw them back into the lake, and watched them swim away; then he looked at Hans Van Doorst.

"Let us bring the net up to dry," Hans said.

They reeled in the windlasses and stretched the soaking seine between them. Ramsay turned for a look at the beach, and he could not see it because the sand was covered with fish. Hans had been right. The bay in front of the Van Hooven home was a very paradise for fish. Countless sturgeon and whitefish lay on the beach. Ramsay heard Hans say, "Now we go to work."

Hans hitched the little horse, brought the cart down to the beach, and began throwing whitefish into it. The bigger, heavier sturgeon, of course, Hans had to lift into the wagon box. When they had a load, he drove to the stacked barrels left by Baptiste LeClaire. Ramsay watched interestedly.

A little trickle of water wound into the lake at this point, and Hans had dammed it in such a fashion that a miniature cataract fell over the stones and mud which he had placed in the water course. Beside this were a big, flat wooden dish, evidently also made by Hans, and several sacks of salt. The Dutchman produced three razor-sharp fish knives, more salvage from the *Spray*, and turned to Pieter. "Do you want to bring the rest of the fish up?"

"Yaah. I'll do that."

Hans caught up a six-pound whitefish and, seeming to use his knife very little, he cut its head off. Leaving the fish unscaled, he sliced it down the backbone to the end of the tail and spilled the viscera out. He washed his fish in the dam's tiny spillway and, filling the wooden dish with salt, he rolled the split whitefish in dry salt. Then he placed it carefully in a two-hundred-pound barrel.

Ramsay caught up a fish and a knife and tried to imitate exactly Hans' procedure. But, though he thought he was doing everything precisely as the Dutchman had done it, he was much slower. Hans had two more fish ready and in the barrel before Ramsay was finished with one. Grimly Ramsay worked on. If this was a part of fishing, it was a part he must and would learn. He picked up another fish and, as he worked, he gained skill.

As soon as one barrel was filled, Hans threw a couple of hands full of salt on top, fitted a head to it and clamped it down with a black ash hoop. Again Ramsay nodded understandingly. He had supposed that a brine solution in which to pack the fish must be prepared, but evidently none was necessary. Enough water remained on the fish to form their own brine. Packed in such a fashion, they would keep for many months.

Pieter brought another load of fish and another, and then set to work with a fish knife to help clean the catch and pack it. The big sturgeon, of course, had to be cut into suitable strips and salted before they were packed. Some of them were filled with roe—caviar—and Pieter carted pails full of that to feed Marta's poultry. The remainder of the waste was loaded into the cart and hauled far away from the scene of the packing. Then Hans scrubbed everything carefully. Fishermen who packed food for human consumption must be very clean.

The sun was down and the moon up before they finished, but when they were done they had packed seven barrels—fourteen hundred pounds—of whitefish and three barrels of sturgeon. It was a rich haul. Though they had worked for almost seventeen hours, each of them had earned more money than the average worker in Devil Chad's tannery received in a full month.

Ramsay sighed as he cleaned and honed his fish knife, and Hans said, "The moon is bright and right for working, and we need a pier."

"A pier?"

"Yaah. Else how will a boat put in to pick our catch up? I work for an hour or so."

Ramsay, thinking of his comfortable bed, stumbled down to the lake to help Hans put in an hour or two on the pier.

CHAPTER EIGHT

ACTION

Restlessly Ramsay picked up a big whitefish and cleaned it. Salting it, he threw the fish into a barrel and picked up another. A freckle-faced urchin about ten years old stood near, watching him. The youngster was Johnny O'Toole, son of Shamus O'Toole. In the summer Shamus did odd jobs. In winter, when boats could not run, he drove one of the sleds that carried leather from Three Points to Milwaukee and cattle hides from Milwaukee to Three Points.

"You goin' to fix a sturgeon?" Johnny demanded.

"Sure," Ramsay said absently. "Pretty soon."

Ramsay's eyes kept straying out on the lake, past the solid wooden pier which Hans, Pieter and Ramsay, had erected. The past days, it seemed, had been nothing but work. Up with the dawn and out to make another catch of fish. Pack the catch, and spend any time that remained working on the pier. Weeds were sprouting as high as the corn, oats were heading untended and unheeded on their stalks, and the farm was getting only the skimpiest attention. All this because they had decided to gamble on fishing.

When the *Jackson*, summoned by Hans, had nosed into their pier, she had taken on board a hundred and twenty barrels—twenty-four thousand pounds of whitefish—and forty thousand pounds of sturgeon. The whitefish, Hans had assured them, would bring not less than five cents a pound in the Chicago market and the sturgeon were worth three cents a pound. When they had their money they would be able to buy a pound net, a pound boat, more salt and barrels, and be ready for fishing on a really big scale.

Ramsay's eyes kept darting toward the lake. The *Jackson's* skipper had said that, depending on how much cargo he had to take on in Chicago and the number of stops between Chicago and Three Points, the ship would be back Tuesday or Wednesday. This was Tuesday, and Ramsay could not control his impatience.

"Fix a sturgeon," Johnny pleaded. "Fix a sturgeon now."

"I ... All right, Johnny."

Ramsay began to dismember a hundred-pound sturgeon, and Johnny O'Toole's eyes danced. He stood anxiously near, trying to remember his manners, but his impatience triumphed. "Gimme his nose, will ya? Can I have his nose?"

"Sure, Johnny."

Ramsay, who had learned a lot about dressing fish since his first halting attempts, sliced the sturgeon's nose off with one clean stroke of his knife. The nose was round as a ball, and as rubbery, and every one of the numberless freckles on Johnny O'Toole's face danced with delight when Ramsay tossed it to him.

Immediately, Johnny began bouncing the sturgeon's nose up and down on the hard-packed ground. He had only to drop it, and the nose bounded higher than his head. This was the rubber ball, and sometimes the only plaything, of children who lived among the commercial fishermen of Lake Michigan. Johnny began throwing the nose against a tree, catching it in his hand as it rebounded to him.

Ramsay—Hans and Pieter were down at the lake, strengthening the pier—picked up another sturgeon and filled a barrel. He sprinkled the usual two handfuls of salt on top of the filled barrel, fitted a head to it, and bound it tightly with a black ash hoop. Ramsay looked at the two sturgeon remaining from this morning's catch, and decided that they would just about fill a barrel. He rolled one of their dwindling supply over.

"Can I have their noses, too?" Johnny begged. "Can I? Huh?"

"Sure, Johnny."

"Gee! Thanks!"

Johnny O'Toole began to play with his four sturgeon noses, sometimes bouncing all of them at once and sometimes juggling them. Ramsay continued to steal glances at the lake. If everything worked out the way Hans said it would, they would have ... Ramsay dared not think of it, but, even after they paid the skipper of the *Jackson* for hauling their catch to Chicago, there would be a great deal.

"I'd better be goin'," Johnny O'Toole said. "My Pa, he whales me if I stay out after dark. Thanks for the sturgeon noses. I can trade two of 'em to my brother for a knife he's got."

"You're welcome, Johnny. Come back when we have some more sturgeon."

"I'll do that!"

Bouncing one of the sturgeon noses ahead of him, Johnny O'Toole started up the beach toward Three Points. Ramsay watched him go, then cleaned the last of the sturgeon, put them in a barrel and sealed it. As the evening shadows lengthened, he looked again at the bay. The *Jackson* still had not put in, and he gave up. The ship would not be here until tomorrow. He left the barrels where they were and went toward the house.

Tradin' Jack Hammersly's four-wheeled cart was again in the yard, its curtains rolled up to reveal the trader's tempting array of wares. His gray horse was in the corral with the little black, and Tradin' Jack Hammersly's stovepipe hat was decorously placed on the bench outside the door. Ramsay grinned faintly as he washed up. The Trader was an eccentric character, and Ramsay suspected that his eccentricities were planned; they made good advertising. But he was likeable, and now they would get more news. Ramsay went into the house.

"Hi, Ramsay," Tradin' Jack greeted him. "How about a pretty ribbon for that girl of yours?"

"I still haven't any girl."

"Slow," Tradin' Jack asserted. "So much time you have spent around here an' still no girl. Too slow."

"I'll get one," Ramsay promised, "but I've been too busy fishing to look the field over."

Tradin' Jack nodded sadly. "Yes. I heard it. That's what I did, heard it. So you go fishin'. So what happens? Can a trader trade fish? No. He can't. Fish you sell in Chicago. Fishermen are the ruination of traders."

"Not everybody will go fishing," Pieter pointed out. "Enough will stay at farming to keep you supplied. Besides, with all the money the fishermen are going to earn, they can buy a lot more of your goods."

"That's so," Tradin' Jack agreed. "That's so, too, but a man's got to take everything into account. If he wants to stay in business, he has to. Got any eggs for me, Marta?"

"Yaah! Crate after crate."

"I'll take 'em. Take 'em all. Fourteen cents a dozen. Fourteen and a half if you'll take it in trade."

His mind on the *Jackson*, which even now should be churning its way toward them, Ramsay only half-listened as Tradin' Jack rattled on about the various events which, combined, went to make up life on the west shore of Lake Michigan. Remembering little of what he had heard, Ramsay went upstairs to bed. Snuggling down into the soft, feather-filled mattress, he tried to stay awake and could not. The work was always too hard and the days too long to forego even one minute's slumber.

The sun was only half-awake when Ramsay got up, breakfasted and went back to the place where they cleaned their fish. Everything that could be was packed and the grounds were clean, but yesterday they had ripped a ragged gash in the seine and now that needed repair. Ramsay, assisted by Hans, set to work with a ball of linen twine. He lost himself in what he was doing. The important thing, if they wanted fish, was to get the net into the water and use it. Even one half-hour must not be wasted.

Ramsay was jerked out of his absorption in the net by two shrill blasts. He sat up, and sprang to his feet as the blasts were repeated. Looking in the direction of the pier, he saw the *Jackson*, her wheel churning up a path of foam, nosing toward the mooring place. Pieter appeared, and Marta. All four raced to the pier, and they reached it before the approaching steamer did. Ramsay and Hans secured mooring lines which a deck hand threw to them, and Captain Williamson of the *Jackson* came down a short ladder.

He was a bustling little man who wore a blue-and-gold uniform which, Ramsay thought, would have graced an admiral in any navy. But he was efficient and he knew the lake. For eleven years he had been running the *Jackson* between Three Points and Chicago without getting her into or even near trouble.

Captain Williamson took a white sheet and a wallet from an inner pocket, and he read from the sheet, "Twenty-four thousand pounds of whitefish you gave me. It brought five cents a pound, or twelve hundred dollars, less a cent a pound for the hauling. Here you are, nine hundred and twenty dollars."

From the wallet he extracted a sheaf of bills and handed them to Hans. Ramsay looked questioningly at him. "The sturgeon?" he asked.

"Ha!" Captain Williamson snorted. "There's enough sturgeon layin' on the Chicago pier to run the whole city for the next six weeks. Nobody's buying it but, since I hauled, I have to be paid. See you later, gentlemen."

Captain Williamson scrambled back up his ladder, which was hauled in after him. Snorting like an overworked draft horse, the *Jackson* backed away from her mooring, made a wide circle into the lake, and puffed on toward Three Points. Ramsay looked incredulously at the money in Hans' fist, slow to realize that, even if they split it among the four of them, it would be more than half a year's wages for each and they had earned it in less than two weeks. Then he looked at Marta's face and burst out laughing.

From the first, Marta had been with them only half-heartedly and only because Pieter could not be swayed from fishing. Now, seeing enough money to buy a farm, and with tangible evidence that fishing paid well, she had swung completely to their side. Pieter and Hans joined in Ramsay's laughter while Marta looked puzzled. She was, as Hans had declared, a good Dutch girl. Definitely she was not avaricious, but no good Dutch girl could fail to be impressed by the sight of so much money. Hans clasped the bills firmly and looked at his partners. "What do you say?" he asked.

"What do you mean?" Ramsay inquired.

"Pound nets we need, pound boats. Men to help us set them. More salt and more barrels. We owe Baptiste. Or shall we divide what we have and keep on fishing with the seine?"

"Will it take so much to buy those things of which you speak?" Marta inquired.

"This and more, if we really want to take fish."

"Then let's do it!" Marta declared.

"Pieter?" Hans inquired.

"Fishing beats farming."

"Ramsay?"

"I came here to fish."

"Come with me."

Hans hitched the little black horse, and Ramsay climbed up on the cart beside him. Captain Klaus, hurrying frantically from his perch atop the house, alighted on the cart and caressed Hans with his bill. The Dutch fisherman whistled happily as he drove along, and Ramsay grinned. This was the way to get things done; work every second of every day to catch fish and then, without even thinking twice about it, invest everything they had earned in more equipment so they could catch even more fish. Captain Klaus winged off the cart to go and see what some of his wild relatives along the lake shore were doing.

Ramsay turned to Hans, "How big is this pound net?"

"Ha! You have never seen one?"

"Never."

"Soon you will. Very soon you will. There are a lot of pieces in each net and, all together, they weigh about six hundred and fifty pounds. It will cost, I think, about thirty cents a pound, or perhaps two hundred dollars for each net. Then we shall need at least one pound boat, and that will cost an additional two hundred dollars. We shall need more rope, perhaps two hundred and fifty pounds, at a cost of about nine cents a pound. Then we shall have to hire men to help us drive spiles for the net. We need more barrels, more salt. The money we have here will provide us with no more than one net."

"How many should we have?"

"I think that you, I and Pieter could handle three on part time. We could very well use seven or eight if we gave full time to pound nets. However, as soon as we get three in working order—and meanwhile we will continue to seine—we will build a good Mackinaw boat, like the *Spray*, and use gill nets, too."

Ramsay whistled. "We're really getting in deep!"

"Ah, yes!" Hans said gleefully. "But the fishing, it is a business! It is the only business for a man!"

Ramsay pondered thoughtfully. Devil Chad, who lately had seemed remote, was now near and his presence could be felt. Probably, to anyone who knew Devil Chad, it would be impossible to go into Three Points without sensing his nearness. If Devil Chad had set out to control everything, then why hadn't he made an attempt to control fishing? Certainly it was profitable. Ramsay dismissed the thought. Maybe Devil Chad had his hands full and lacked the time to intrude on the fisheries. It still seemed strange that he would lack time to intrude on anything that offered an honest, or even a dishonest, dollar.

Captain Klaus came winging back to the cart and perched on the Dutchman's shoulder. Hans turned the little horse down a dim road, one Ramsay had not yet noticed, on the edge of Three Points, and they came out on the borders of a river that emptied into the lake.

There was a large shed with a chimney that leaned at a crazy angle and belched a thin trickle of smoke. Hans halted the little horse, who immediately lowered his head to nibble at one of the few patches of green grass growing on this sand beach. Ramsay turned his head to look at the place.

Lumber of various sizes and cuts was stacked all about it, and there was a pile of uncut logs left to season. Ramsay saw the gleam of a saw and caught the scent of a wood-fired boiler. Now the saw's shrill roar was stilled and the boiler's fires were banked. Ramsay looked at the dozen boats that were drawn up on the river bank. They were sturdy, fourteen to sixteen feet long, and propelled wholly by oars. At the back of each was sort of a small winch. There were broad seats and long oars. Ramsay turned to face the man who emerged from the shed.

He was tall, blond and so big that he was almost fat. But his quick eyes were not those of a dull-witted fat man, and his big hands tapered into slim, expressive, artist's fingers. A ready smile seemed engraved on his thick lips, and his blue eyes lighted readily. "Hans!" he exclaimed.

"Hello, Tom," Hans said.

"What the dickens! I thought you'd gone off some place!"

Hans laughed. "Not me! I wish you to meet one of my new partners, Ramsay Cartou. Ramsay, Tom Nedley. He is an artist with the wood and could make fine violins, but he prefers to pass his time on this river bank, making pound boats for indigent fishermen."

"Glad to know you." Tom wrung Ramsay's hand. "What are you up to?"

"We have come," Hans announced, "to get a pound boat."

"Sure. Take your pick."

"We," Hans said grandly, "have the money to pay for it."

"Gosh! I heard you lost the *Spray*?"

"That we did," Hans conceded, "and three good men with it. But we shall build another boat as good. Can you, by the way, supply me with a good oaken keel and cedar planking?"

"Sure. I'll even show you where there's some big cedar stumps that'll do for the ribbing."

"I already know," Hans said. "What we wish to have you do now is deliver a good pound boat to Pieter Van Hooven's place. Two hundred dollars?"

"Yup. But if you haven't the money ..."

"We have it," Hans assured him. He counted out some money and pressed it into Tom Nedley's hands. The big boatmaker looked both embarrassed and pleased. "Gosh! Thanks! Got your spiles driven?"

"Nope."

"For that you need two boats."

"Of that I am aware. But we do not have money to buy two."

"I'll get my brother, my cousin and their sons," Tom Nedley offered. "Be down in the mornin'."

"For that we will pay you."

"Aw, Hans ..."

"Take it." Hans grinned. "We are certain to get rich fishing but, if we don't, you will have something."

"Aw shucks ..."

"Take it!"

"We'll be there."

"Thanks," Hans said.

Mounting the cart, he turned the horse around and at a smart trot drove up into the village. Ramsay sat proudly erect, feeling strength like that of a young bull arise within him. This was the village from which he had been driven in disgrace by Devil Chad, but it was a village he dared return to. Any time he felt like it he would return to Three Points, and let Devil Chad meet him if he dared. Hans stopped the horse in front of a cottage which might have been an exact duplicate of the one occupied by Pierre and Madame LeDou.

Letting the horse stand, Hans leaped from the cart and faced Ramsay. "This," he announced loudly, "is the home of Frog-Mouth Fontan, whose good wife is about to sell us a pound net. Frog-Mouth, by the way, is one of Devil Chad's closest friends."

As though summoned by the voice, one of the very few tall Frenchmen Ramsay had ever seen appeared at the door. His mouth, the boy noticed, was oddly like that of a frog. As soon as he recognized his visitor, he emitted an enraged bellow and charged.

Hans grinned, stepped aside, and swung. But Frog-Mouth Fontan was an expert fighter, too. He dodged, pivoted and dealt two swift blows that set Hans' head to rocking. Then the Dutchman found the range, and sent his pile-driver fist into Frog-Mouth's jaw. He hit again, and a third time. Frog-Mouth Fontan staggered, weaved backwards, and with a silly grin on his face sat down against the cabin. He continued to grin foolishly, staring into the bright sun. A small, dark woman without any teeth appeared at the door. She looked at her husband, then spat at him. "*Cochon!*" she said. "Pig!" She looked at Ramsay and Hans. "What do you want?"

"One of your excellent pound nets, Madame Fontan," Hans murmured politely.

"Do you have the money to pay for it?"

"We have it."

"Load the net."

Ramsay helped Hans lift the folded net, four pieces of three-and-a-quarter-inch webbing, two pieces of six-and-a-quarter-inch, and seven pieces of eight-and-a-half-inch, onto the cart. The latter sagged beneath almost seven hundred pounds of net, and the little horse looked questioningly around. But he stepped out obediently when Hans slapped the reins over his back, and Captain Klaus squawked over them as they returned to Pieter's farm.

The next morning Ramsay stared in astonishment at a unique craft coming down the lake. Five men, one of whom was Tom Nedley, manned the outlandish rigging, and it was propelled by two sets of oars. Ramsay strolled down to meet it, and noticed some spiles—poles—about thirty-five feet long, that were piled on the beach. Evidently Hans had cut them, or had them brought down, after he and Ramsay returned home. The craft, and as it drew near, Ramsay saw that it was two sixteen-foot pound boats, bound together by stout planks front and rear, nosed into the pier. The crew disembarked, and Tom Nedley introduced Ramsay to his brother, his cousin and their two strapping sons. Ramsay turned a curious gaze on the boats.

They were lashed solidly together by planks that kept them about fifteen feet apart. On top of the planks was raised a sort of scaffolding, connected by a heavy beam whose nether surface was about twenty feet from the water. Suspended from the beam was a four-pulley block with a rope through each pulley, and the ropes supported an iron drop hammer. There was another pulley whose use Ramsay could not even guess.

Shouting and scrambling as though this were some sort of picnic especially arranged just for them, Tom Nedley's boisterous crew threw the spiles in the water and floated them out to the boats. They tied them to the stern, then set up a concerted shouting. "Hans! Hey, Hans! Pieter!"

Grinning, Hans and Pieter, who had lingered over their breakfast after Ramsay was finished, appeared from the house. Tom Nedley's brother said plaintively, "Twenty minutes of six! Half the day gone already! Don't you fellows ever do anything except sleep?"

"Yaah!" Hans scoffed. "Who is so filled with ambition?" He looked at the oarsman who had spoken and leaped lightly into the boat. "Now we will see who is the best man."

Ramsay jumped on board just in time to keep from being left behind, and Hans bent his mighty back to the oars. In the second boat the other oarsman tried to match Hans' pace, and the unwieldy craft spurted away like a frightened deer. Trailing behind, the spiles left a path of bubbly ripples.

Out of the bay they went and into the open lake. Then they turned south, obviously Hans had some destination in mind. At any rate, he seemed to know exactly where he was going. They stopped rowing on a reef about a mile from shore, and one of the men retrieved a spile.

Tom Nedley spoke to Ramsay. "Feel strong?"

"Sure thing."

"Good. We'll need some strong men around here. Wait until they're set, an' then I'll show you what to do."

Hans and another man up-ended the spile and probed toward the lake bottom with it. They hung it on the other pulley and, when it was in place, the end was about three feet below the drop-hammer. Hans fastened it to the pulley, steadied it with his hands and sang out, "Let her go!"

Tom Nedley handed a long rope to Ramsay, bade him hold it tight, and two men in the other boat took the other two ropes. Jerking the rope in his hands, Tom Nedley tripped the latch holding the drop-hammer, and instantly Ramsay felt the weight.

He hung on very tightly and was reassured by Tom Nedley's quiet, "You'll soon get the hang of it. When I give the word, let the hammer fall just hard enough to hit the spile. Stop it, of course, before it hits the boys steadyin' for us."

Ramsay waited, his eyes on Tom Nedley. The big man said, "Now!"

The hammer dropped squarely but not completely, because Ramsay tried to stop it too soon. Again Tom Nedley reassured him.

"Just let her fall," he urged, as he helped raise the hammer back into position. "There's plenty of time to stop her, but don't be careless. That hammer weighs a hundred and seventy five pounds, an' I doubt if even Hans' head would take that much fallin' on it."

This time Ramsay got the rhythm. The hammer dropped swiftly, squarely and with full force. It seated the spile in the lake bottom, so that there was no longer any necessity for holding it. Hans and the other stepped back. Again and again Ramsay helped drop the hammer, until the pole was driven about eight feet into the lake bottom and perhaps four feet remained above the surface. It had been about thirty-six feet to start with, therefore the water at this place was twenty-four feet deep. It should be right for whitefish.

"Let me take that rope a while," someone said.

Gladly Ramsay relinquished his rope to Pieter, and rested his aching shoulders while he watched interestedly. The piles were being driven in a geometrical pattern, a sort of square, and Ramsay understood that the first nine were to hold the pot, the actual trap. Measuring carefully, the boats moved away and more spiles were driven. These were for the hearts of the net. Finally, running straight toward shore, spiles were driven in a pattern that resembled the forks of a 'Y.' To these would be attached the tunnel, the webbing that guided fish through the hearts of the pound net and into the pot.

Ramsay straightened, easing his aching shoulders. It was hard work, very hard, to lift the hammer and let it fall for hours on end. But now the spiles for one pound net were driven. The boy turned to Hans. "Gee whiz! How about moving all this?"

"You don't move a pound net except, of course, to take up the webbing when the lake freezes. Otherwise, we'll leave this right where it is. It is possible to fish a pound net in the same location for fifty years or more."

"What's next?"

"Set the net. I think there is still time."

They rowed back to the pier, where Marta, who had taken over the treasurer's post, paid Tom Nedley and his crew. The big man grinned his thanks.

"You need us again, you know where to find us."

"We'll probably take you up on that," Hans said.

The ropes binding the two boats were loosened and the scaffold taken down. Leaving the boat Hans had bought, Tom Nedley and his helpers piled into the other one and started rowing up the lake. Hans, Pieter and Ramsay went to the pound net.

The pot, the trap, was loaded first. Then came the flaring, heart-shaped 'hearts,' and finally the leads, or tunnel. Setting himself to the oars, Hans rowed back to where they had driven the piles. He tied the lead, the beginning of the tunnel, to the spile. A five-pound stone fastened to the bottom rope carried it down into the lake. Giving the oars to Ramsay and cautioning him to travel slowly, Hans fastened the lead to each spile and sank it with stones. The flaring hearts were set in the same way.

Coming to the pot, Hans first fastened a four-foot chain with an attached pulley to the pile. Then he tied a rope, double the depth of the water and with some allowance for shrinkage, to the bottom of the pot. He did this on each spile, and they put the whole pot into the water. Ramsay began to understand.

In effect, they had set a gigantic fly-trap. Any fish that came along would be guided by the tunnel into the hearts, and then into the pot. Should any escape, the flaring sides of the hearts would keep them trapped and, nine times out of ten, send them back into the pot instead of out through the tunnel.

Ramsay labored under the weight of a two-hundred-pound sturgeon which had been dragged in by the seine. Hans and Pieter hadn't wanted to bother with sturgeon because there was no market for them, anyhow, but Ramsay had permitted them to throw none back into the lake. Cradling his slippery prize across his chest, as though it was a log, he carried it to the pond and threw it in. For a moment the sturgeon swam dazedly on the surface, then flipped his tail and submerged. Ramsay gazed into the pond. It was alive with sturgeon weighing from seventy-five to almost three hundred pounds. There were so many that, to supplement the food in the pond, they were feeding them ground corn.

Ramsay stripped off his wet clothes and dived cleanly into the pond. Water surged about him, washing off all the sweat and grime which he had accumulated during the day. He probed along the pond's bottom, and felt the smooth sides of a sturgeon beneath him. It was only a little one.

He swam on until he had to surface for air, and dived again. Across the pond's murky depths he prowled, his white body gleaming like some great worm in the water. Finally he found what he was looking for.

It was a big sturgeon, and it was feeding quietly. Moving as slowly as possible, Ramsay rubbed a hand across its back. Suddenly he wrapped both arms about the fish and took a firm grasp with his bare legs.

For a moment, while the dull sturgeon tried to determine what was happening, there was no movement. Then the big fish awakened to danger and shot to the surface. With all the speed of an outboard motor he sliced along it, and a moment later he dived again. Grinning, exhilarated, Ramsay swam back to shore and dressed.

Tradin' Jack Hammersly's rig was in the yard, and Ramsay heard the man say, "Marta, what you been feedin' your hens?"

"The best!" Marta said indignantly. "The very best!"

"The best of what?"

"Why grain, and scraps, and ..."

"And sturgeon roe?"

"Why—yes."

"What I thought," Tradin' Jack sighed. "Ye'll have to stop it. Ever' customer as got some of your eggs told me they taste like caviar!"

A moment later there was a rapid-fire sputter of French expletives. His face red, seeming about to explode, Baptiste LeClaire raced around the corner of the house.

"Get your guns!" he screamed when he saw Ramsay. "Get your knives and clubs too! Get everything! We have to kill everybody!"

CHAPTER NINE

PIRATES

Baptiste was dancing up and down, flinging his arms like the blades of a windmill and screaming in French. Ramsay wrinkled his brow. He had picked up some French, but not enough to translate the torrent of words that rolled out of the agitated man's mouth. And never before in his life had he seen anyone so mad. Baptiste was invoking every evil he could think of, a most generous portion, upon someone's hapless head. Ramsay made a move to stop him.

"Wait. I can't follow you...."

A few English words, among which Ramsay recognized pig, dog and son of a rotten fish, mingled with Baptiste's violent Gallic tirade. He continued to wave his arms and yell. Ramsay waited helplessly, unable to understand or to do anything. Attracted by the clamor, Hans, Pieter, Marta and Tradin' Jack appeared.

Very quietly Hans advanced to Baptiste's side. "What is it, my friend?"

Almost tearfully, grateful because, at last, he had someone able to understand, Baptiste turned his machine-gun rattle of French on Hans. Ramsay watched the Dutch fisherman's face tighten, and then it was set in white-hot anger. He waited for Baptiste to finish, and asked in English, "Do you know who did it?"

"No." Having worn himself out, Baptiste lapsed naturally into English, too. He turned his hot, angry face on the others.

Hans spoke again. "Go to Madame Fontan in Three Points," he said to Baptiste. "Tell her that I, Hans Van Doorst, said that you are to have the nets you need. If she has not enough woven, get them elsewhere. Madame LeDou makes excellent seines and gill nets. Go to the store for the rope you need, and tell them I will pay for everything. We ourselves will come to help you drive new spiles and make new sets."

"It is good of you," Baptiste's face was still flaming with rage, "but we cannot let the matter rest there."

"Nor can we," Hans' tone was calm and reasoning, "go about shooting people when we do not know who to shoot."

"Pah! I know! It is Devil Chad!"

"Have you proof of that?"

"The proof is self-evident. Who but Devil Chad would dare do such a thing?"

"Did you see him?"

"Does one see the wise fox when he comes in the night to steal a fat goose? No, I did not see him."

"Listen, my friend. Listen carefully. If this sort of piracy has been started and we do not end it, we are lost. But ours will be a small triumph if all of us get ourselves hanged. We must proceed with caution."

"I do not like caution."

"Nevertheless, we must now employ it. We cannot rush off with guns and shoot because we suspect. Get your nets and whatever else you need, and start anew. When you can bring me proof of the pirates, I myself will be the first to shoot."

"It is the stumbling way."

"It is the only way. If there is to be war, then let there be war. But we cannot strike out blindly. To do that will be to turn every man's hand against us. We cannot fight at all if we do not know our enemies."

For a moment the dark-visaged little Frenchman stood uncertainly. Then he looked directly at Hans. "I will do as you say," he agreed. "But should I catch anyone at my nets, they or I will not live to speak of it afterwards."

"The same will happen should I catch anyone at our nets," Hans promised. "But let us catch them before we act."

Baptiste LeClaire swept his hat off, made a courtly bow, murmured, "Your health, Madame and Messieurs," and turned back toward the pier. Expertly handled, the *Bon Homme* sailed gracefully into the lake. Astonished, Ramsay stared at Hans, and Pieter and Marta reflected his astonishment.

"What's got him by the ear?" Ramsay asked.

"Baptiste," Hans said, "had three pound nets which he tended with pound boats. He had a number of gill nets which he visited with the *Bon Homme*, a proper gill net boat."

Hans stared out on the lake, as though seeking the answer to some question that plagued him. He turned to face the others.

"Baptiste has no more pound nets. They have all been raised and ripped to shreds. The spiles to which he attached them were broken. Of the gill nets he once had, one remains. The rest were destroyed. Aside from his years of labor, Baptiste has lost more than two thousand dollars' worth of nets."

"Who did it?" Ramsay gasped.

Hans shrugged. "Someone who has discovered, at last, that there is money to be had in Lake Michigan fishing. Someone who will stop at nothing to get all of it for himself."

There was conviction in Ramsay's "Devil Chad!"

Hans shrugged again. "So Baptiste thinks."

"What do you think?"

Hans swung so fiercely on him that Ramsay retreated a step. "You heard what I told Baptiste!" the Dutch fisherman said. "We must be certain! It is not for us to appoint ourselves judge, jury and executioner! Before we act we must be sure!"

"Should we call in the constable?"

Hans said scornfully, "Devil Chad's man!"

"What must we do?"

"Watch ourselves," Hans declared. "Hereafter we must leave the nets unguarded and the lake without our own patrol, only when we are sure it is safe. If someone has come to take from us our right to fish, we must be our own protection. At the same time we must not act blindly. The lake is big enough for all. If one has come who would take everything for himself, we fight."

"You know it's Devil Chad."

"I know no such thing."

"Do you suspect him?"

"Yes," Hans answered frankly.

"Then why not take action?"

"Look, boy," and Ramsay writhed because never before had Hans addressed him in such a fashion, "lives are now at stake. Let us be sure before we lose ours or take someone else's!"

"You are right," Pieter approved. "Yes, you are right."

Puzzled, Ramsay looked at his two partners. It was absurd to suppose that either was afraid; they had proven their courage too many times. Yet, though both thought Devil Chad the raider, both refused to move against him until they had proof of his piracies. Ramsay thought of something he had read, 'A man is innocent until proven guilty.' Maybe Hans and Pieter believed that sincerely, while the hot-headed Baptiste was ready to strike at anything at all.

Ramsay felt a rising admiration for his partners. "What must we do?" he asked.

"I doubt if they'll strike by day," Hans said. "If they come, it will be in the night. We'll make three watches, and alternate on them. That way they cannot surprise us."

"Suppose they come?"

Hans shrugged eloquently. "Then we will fight and fight hard, for it is certain that no one else will do our fighting for us. Do either of you have a choice as to watches?"

Nobody had a choice. Hans broke three straws of different lengths, concealed them in the palm of his hand, and held them out. They drew, and compared straws. Pieter had the shortest, the first watch, Ramsay the second and Hans the third. Hans looked thoughtfully at the twilight-softened lake. "Pieter, do you want to go out at seven and stay until eleven?"

"Yaah."

"Good. Ramsay, stay out until about two and awaken me."

"All right."

Ramsay ate the excellent supper Marta had prepared, listened idly to the chatter of Tradin' Jack, who knew what had happened and was nervous because of it, and went upstairs to bed. In spite of his inner tension and his excitement, his head had scarcely touched the pillow when he dozed off. A moment later, or so it seemed, Pieter was touching his shoulder.

"It's time."

"I ... Huh? Oh, yes."

Ramsay came fully awake, and Pieter lighted the candle in his room. Its beams sparkled brightly on the shining barrel of the muzzle-loading fowling-piece Pieter carried. Of a huge bore, the gun was charged with black powder and loaded with lead slugs. Ramsay shuddered as he accepted it. Such a gun would be sure to work great havoc among anything it was shot at, but its recoil alone would probably set a mule back on its haunches.

"Anything happen?" Ramsay whispered.

"Nothing," Pieter said. "Nobody came. The lake is calm and the boat awaits you on the beach."

"I'll see you in the morning."

"Good luck."

His shoes in one hand and the shotgun in the other, Ramsay stole quietly down the stairs and out the back door. He stopped to put his shoes on, and looked around him.

A pale moon shone through disheveled clouds that gave the sky the appearance of a man sadly in need of a hair-cut, and the faintest suspicion of a breeze kicked up small wavelets. Asleep on the ridge pole, Captain Klaus was a dull, shapeless blob in the night sky. Ramsay cradled the shotgun in his right elbow and walked down to the beach.

The pound boat had wedged itself lightly against the sand. Ramsay put the anchor back in, carefully laid the shotgun on the rower's seat, and stood in the stern until he had tilted the craft from its mooring. Sitting down, with a vigorous stroke of the oars he sent the boat farther into the lake.

In the bay a fish jumped out of water, and the sound of its falling back made a tinkling splash. Ramsay, dipping his oars quietly, steered toward the first pound net they had set. At intervals he halted to rest on the oars. There were no sounds save those that should have been present. Except for him and the pound boat, the lake seemed deserted. Lingering in the shadows, Ramsay circled the net and saw nothing. He started toward another of their pound nets.

They had kept the seine busy, taken good catches from their pound nets, and turned most of their money back into additional equipment. They were getting ahead and setting themselves up in the fishing business. By next year they should have everything they needed. They would not have to buy any nets, or boats, and could begin to enjoy the profits they were earning.

Ramsay found himself thinking of Devil Chad. Fishing was very hard work, and expensive, but whoever did it well could hope for a fine future. Lake Michigan was a vast reservoir of riches, and they were to be used. There was room for all, but so was there room in Three Points. Devil Chad wanted that for himself. Who but Devil Chad could now be plotting to seize the Lake Michigan fisheries?

Ramsay shrugged such thoughts away. Out here on the lake he seemed able to think with great clarity, and he knew that Hans and Pieter were right. They must not lash out in thoughtless anger and hit at Devil Chad because he was the logical one to raid their nets. They must have proof, and strike as hard as possible when they struck.

Ramsay visited all three pound nets, and rowed back to the first one. The lake remained calm and unruffled. When he thought it was two o'clock—the night was divided into one watch of four hours and two of three each—he went in to rouse Hans. At half-past five, when they ate breakfast, Hans had nothing to report. If pirates were out to get all nets, certainly they had not bothered theirs.

Late that afternoon, when the fishing was done and Ramsay, much to the amusement of Hans and Pieter, had carried six more big sturgeon to the pond, Hans hitched the black horse and invited Ramsay to go with him to Three Points. Captain Klaus, as usual, flew to the back of the cart and perched where he could caress Hans with his bill. Hans turned the little horse down the road leading to Tom Nedley's. Ramsay stirred with interest.

Big Tom Nedley came out of his shed, greeted them, and looked doubtfully at the little cart. He glanced from it to a long oaken beam that was supported on wooden horses. When he looked again at Hans, his voice and manner were almost accusing. "You aim to drag that piece of oak?"

"You think I'm a fool?" Hans challenged.

"Didn't think you'd drag it." Tom Nedley seemed relieved. "There ain't another piece of oak like that one in Wisconsin. How do you aim to get it home?"

"You have an extra pair of wheels and an axle?"

"Sure, but ..."

"Ha! Bring me a wrench!"

The wrench in his hands, Hans set to work unbolting the clamps that held the body on Pieter's two-wheeled cart. He lifted the body and seat off, leaving the horse hitched only to the wheels and the axle that joined them.

Hans looked triumphantly at Tom Nedley, and the boatbuilder scratched his head. "You needn't think you're so smart. I'd of thought of that myself afore I let you drag that timber."

"Why didn't you?"

While Tom brought another pair of wheels, Ramsay looked at the solid chunk of oak. About twenty-six feet long, it was very fine-grained and it hadn't a crack or flaw throughout its length—fully seasoned, so that not a drop of sap remained in it. Even Ramsay, whose knowledge of wood was limited, could tell that this was an exceptionally fine chunk of oak. Hans and Tom Nedley seemed to look upon it as they would have looked upon some valuable jewel. Hans patted it affectionately.

"Stronger than steel!" he said fondly. "Can you not imagine what a boat the *Spray II* will be?"

Tom Nedley said, "Building from that, you cannot fail."

For a moment Hans was wistful, as though he had gone back in memory to the first *Spray*.

Tom Nedley brought another set of wheels, rolled them into place, and covered the bare axle with a soft blanket. He used another blanket to pad the axle to which the horse was hitched, and Hans steered the horse into position. Hans, Tom and Ramsay lifted one end of the oaken beam onto the rear wheels. Ramsay helped lift the other end onto the other set of wheels, and stood aside while Hans lashed both with ropes.

Ramsay watched interestedly. Hans used his ropes to permit flexibility, while at the same time he took no chances on their chafing or breaking. Apparently fishermen could do anything with ropes. Ramsay tied the unbolted seat and body to the top of the oaken beam. Hans took the little horse's bridle and led him carefully back to the road. Mounted on its four wheels, the long oaken beam swayed and turned.

Leading the little horse, careful of everything that lay in front, behind and on both sides, Hans set a very slow pace. It was as though the beam were a very fragile thing that might break should it brush even the smallest tree. Actually, if it hit one hard, it would have broken any small tree in its path and rocked the larger ones. Hans continued to treat it as though it were a very delicate thing.

Destined to be the keel of the *Spray II*, when they reached Pieter's house the beam was lovingly set up on three scaffoldings made of four-by-sixes and arranged near the lake. Hans patted it as lovingly as he would have stroked a favorite dog. "We have a start!" he said happily.

"Why do we need another boat?" Ramsay queried.

"For setting gill nets," Hans replied. "You are not a fisherman unless you know how to set a gill net, and you cannot set a gill net unless you have a proper Mackinaw boat." He petted the oaken beam again. "As responsive as a canoe it shall be, but as strong as a pound boat! This one shall not break no matter what happens. The lake will not breed a storm that it will be unable to ride out."

That night Ramsay's was the first watch. He rowed the pound boat from one to another of their three pound nets. No strange vessel disturbed the lake, no hostile creature approached. Ramsay gave his watch over to Hans, and slept until dawn. They fished, processed their catch and loaded thirty thousand pounds of whitefish onto the *Jackson* when she nosed into their pier.

Ramsay went with Hans and Pieter to a place where some mighty cedar trees, that had grown for centuries, had been cut when the snow was deep. Their weathered stumps thrust six feet or more above the green foliage that surrounded them, and Hans chose very carefully. He wanted only those stumps with a fine, closely knit grain, those which, even in death, showed no cracks or flaws. He found three of which he approved, and Ramsay and Pieter used a cross-cut saw to cut them off very close to the earth. Ramsay began to understand the project in Hans' mind.

Because of weather conditions, pound nets, at the very most, could be used for only about three to four months out of every year. The seine, though under no circumstances would Hans fish in the spawning season, could be dragged in until the bay froze. But gill nets could be used for seven or eight months if one had a proper boat, and Hans wanted to build one that would ride out any storm.

It was not to be an ordinary Mackinaw boat, but one such as Lake Michigan had never seen. Its oaken keel had been chosen with an eye to the heaviest seas and the ice that speckled those seas in spring or fall. Though some fishermen used cedar planking for the ribbing of their boats, and steamed it until it could be bent into the desired shape, Hans intended to cut his directly from cedar stumps that had already endured five hundred years and ten thousand storms. Then the *Spray II* would be sheathed with the best possible cedar planking and calked with the best obtainable oakum, or rope soaked in tar.

They would not float her this season. Neither effort nor expense were to be spared in the building of the *Spray II*, and constructing her properly would be a winter's job. But as soon as the ice broke next year she would be ready to float, and they would be ready to set their gill nets.

Ramsay grinned fleetingly as he tossed bushels of ground corn into the pond so that the numerous sturgeon he had imprisoned there would have enough to eat. It seemed so very long ago that he had thrown in with Hans and Pieter and decided to become a fisherman, and he still hadn't two silver dollars to jingle in his pocket. Not one day, scarcely one hour had been free of grueling labor. But they had two pound boats, three pound nets, had bought another seine, and with spring they would have the *Spray II*. In addition, there was enough of the season left, so that they should be able to catch plenty of fish before either ice or the spawning period curtailed operations. That would give them enough money to buy gill nets, as well as anything else they needed. None of the four partners would come out of this season with money in their pockets. They would own a sufficient amount of equipment for next year, and much of what they earned then would be profit.

That night Ramsay took the third watch. He rowed softly from one pound net to the other, always keeping in the shadows so that there was small danger of his being noticed. He had been out about an hour, and had two more to go, when he saw a boat approaching.

It came from the north, Three Points, and its row locks were so well greased that not the faintest sound came from them. The oarsman was expert; he dipped and raised his oars so that there was no splashing. Ramsay raised the shot gun. He leveled it.

Unseen by the other boatmen, he lurked in the shadows and let them pass. Ramsay was somewhat surprised to see them give a pound net a wide berth and head into the bay. He followed, rowing his own boat silently while he tried to discern the others' intentions. There were at least four, and perhaps five, men in the other boat and they were going toward the pier. Ramsay let them draw ahead, then circled around them and as fast as he could without making any noise, he rowed straight toward the beach. Grounding his boat, he stepped out. He was aware of the other boat being drawn up cautiously.

He walked toward the nocturnal visitors until he was within a half-dozen rods. He could see them now, clustered about the pier. Two started for the barrels and the barreled fish. There was a faint whispering. Ramsay waited to hear no more.

Had these people been well-intentioned, they would not be so secretive. Plainly they were up to no good.

Ramsay pointed the shotgun toward the sky—he had no wish to kill anyone—braced the stock against his shoulder, and pressed the trigger. The gun belched its load of leaden pellets, and red flame flashed from the muzzle. Ramsay shouted as loudly as he could. "Pieter! Hans!"

Dropping the shotgun on the sand beach, he rushed forward. The two men who had started toward the barrels and barreled fish came running back. Ramsay glared his anger.

Though he could not be positive because it was too dark to identify anything or anyone positively, he thought that the man who stood just a little to one side of the rest was Joe Mannis, the body-watcher. Ramsay swerved toward him, sent his doubled fist into the other's stomach, and heard a mighty 'whoosh' as he knocked the wind out of his enemy. Up at the house a door slammed.

Then a club or blackjack collided soddenly with the side of Ramsay's head and set him reeling. He stumbled forward, feeling a little foolish because all the strength had left him. Without being sure that he did so, he sat down on the sand and blinked owlishly at the night visitors. Dimly he was aware of the fact that they were launching their boat and that he must stop them, but he did not know how to do so.

A nightgown flapping about his legs and a tasseled red cap on his head, Hans Van Doorst appeared on the beach. A pair of trousers hastily strapped about his own nightgown, Pieter followed. Both men looked quietly at the retreating boat, which they might have followed and would have followed had not Ramsay needed help. They lifted him to his feet.

"What happened?" Hans asked quietly.

"I ... They came while I was out on the lake, but they didn't bother the nets. They rowed right into the pier, and I don't know what they wanted."

"Did you recognize any of them?"

"I think Joe Mannis was one."

"Devil Chad?"

Ramsay said positively, "He was not among them. I would have recognized him."

"Did you shoot at them?"

"No, I shot to attract you and Pieter."

"Well, that's all right, too. They won't be back tonight, or likely any other night. Come on."

They helped Ramsay into the house, bathed his head and put him to bed. He awoke to a mist-filled morning.

No breath of air stirred. Visibility was almost non-existent; the mist was so heavy that it almost hid the lake. Ramsay, with all the elasticity of youth, had recovered quickly from last night's incident and he had a good appetite for the breakfast Marta had prepared.

Then Marta tossed her head defiantly. "All of you have been away," she announced, "and you have done many things. I have been nowhere and I have not done anything. But today I go to Three Points to shop."

"Sure," Pieter said. "I'll hitch the horse for you."

They cheered Marta on her way and went down to cast the seine. The pound nets, having been visited within the past two days, would not again be visited today. Aside from that, they had seined tons of whitefish and sturgeon out of the bay in front of Pieter's house. Naturally the catches were growing smaller. If they didn't take the seine too far out, and set it shallow, three men could work the windlasses.

Then, just as they were ready to fish, and just about when Marta should have reached Three Points, a man on a lathered horse came pounding down the sand beach. He drew his tired mount up. "Quick!" he gasped. "An accident! Marta is badly hurt!"

CHAPTER TEN

THE GREAT FISH

The great White Sturgeon was not, in the truest sense of the word, a native of the lake. More years ago than any living thing could remember, he had been born, along with thousands of brothers and sisters, halfway up one of the many rivers that emptied into the lake. The sturgeon remembered little about that time, but just the same it had helped to shape him and make him what he was.

The spawning sturgeon, a vast number of them, had started up the river together. It was a journey as old as the lake itself. Side by side they swam, in such numbers and so many evenly-spaced layers that none of the many Indians who fished along the river was able to thrust his spear without striking a sturgeon. Preying bears, otter, panthers, lynx and other creatures that liked fish, thronged the river's banks and struck at the horde as it passed. So little did all their raids combined matter that it was as though they had taken nothing. No creature that wanted one lacked a sturgeon to eat. But the great mass of fish, impelled by the desperate necessity of laying their eggs in the river, swam on.

Only when miles were behind them and they were about a third of the way to the river's source, did the vast schools start to thin out. Then it was not because their enemies took too many, though they caught a great number. The schools started to lessen because many, too exhausted to go farther or content with spawning grounds already reached, dropped behind to spawn.

Finally only a few, not necessarily the biggest but invariably the most vigorous, were left. Day after day, night after night, stopping only to rest or feed, they went on up the virgin river. Buck deer, drinking, saw the fleeting shadows pass, snorted and leaped skittishly away. Drinking buffalo raised their shaggy heads and, with water dribbling from their muzzles, stared after the migrating fish.

Everything seemed, in some small way, to sense the mystery that went with the swimming sturgeon. They were part of the abundance of this wealthy land, and when they were through spawning, that abundance would be increased. The very presence of the fish was within itself a promise that more were to follow.

Finally there were only half a dozen sturgeon left.

One was a very strong female whose spawn-swollen body even now contained the egg, the cell, that was to be the great White Sturgeon. Swimming close beside her was an equally vigorous male. All the sturgeon that had been able to come this far were among the finest and best.

They stopped in a quiet pool which, within itself, was almost a little lake. A third of a mile wide by a mile and a half long, the pool rolled smoothly down an almost level course. It was shaded on either side by gloomy pines that marched like soldiers in disordered rank for a very great distance. There were no grunting buffalo here, though an occasional white-tailed deer tripped daintily down to drink from the sweet, unpolluted water.

On either side of the pool was a mat of green sedges and water-lilies, and in them a great horde of ducks were rearing their young. They skittered foolishly over the water, seeming to pay no attention to anything save the sheer joy of being alive. Now and then the water beneath them would dimple and ripple in widening circles towards either bank; and when it did, invariably there would be one less duckling. Nothing paid any attention whatever to such casualties. Life teemed in the pool, and there life also fed on life. It was meant to be, and the mighty pike that lived in the pool had to eat, too.

Weary, but far from exhausted, the female carrying the White Sturgeon-to-be pushed herself into the sedges and lay quietly while she rid herself of the burden that she had carried so far. A million or more eggs she left there, and almost before she was finished two little pike that made their home in the sedges had started gobbling them up.

The female sturgeon paid absolutely no attention, and neither did her mate, when he came to fertilize the eggs. They were here to do, and knew how to do, only one thing. Finished, they had no thought as to what might happen next. The two sturgeon swam back into the pool and rested before beginning their long return journey to the great lake. But they had chosen wisely and well.

Almost before the parent fish left, a mink that had long had his eye on the small pike swam quietly down to take one while it was feeding. The other one fled. Though other things came to eat them, in due time what remained of the spawn hatched. The White Sturgeon was the first to appear.

The baby fish came of strong parents, so that there were almost no infertile eggs, but such inroads had already been made among them that not one in twenty ever knew life. Immediately they were singled out by hungry enemies.

The White Sturgeon should have died first for, though all his brothers and sisters were almost the color of the water in which they found birth, he was distinctly different. He was lighter—perhaps a throwback to some distant age when all sturgeon were white—and thus he was the easiest to see. But he seemed to have been born with compensating factors.

When a foot-long bass, a very monster of a thing compared with the baby sturgeon, swam among them, they scattered in wild panic. The feeding bass had only to snap here and there to get all he wanted, but the White Sturgeon did not flee with the rest. Instead, he sank down beside a cattail and did not move. A tiny cloud of mud-colored water drifted around and covered him.

Thus, from the very first, the White Sturgeon seemed to have a keener brain, or a sharper instinct, that made up for his distinctive coloring. Though he should have been the first to die, he did not die. He learned his lessons well, and saw how many of his brothers and sisters perished. Thus he discovered how to stay alive.

For weeks he lived near his birthplace, swimming scarcely two yards from it and feeding on minute particles of both vegetable and animal life. Most of his time he spent feeding, and he grew very fast. Not until encroaching winter drove him there did he move out into the pool.

Most of the ducks were gone before the first thin shell ice formed on the borders of the pool, and those that lingered after that flew out with the first snow. The snow blew in from the north on the heels of an unseasonably early winter wind, and the White Sturgeon saw the mighty pines heaped with feathery snow. Snow lay deep on the ground, and the deer that came down to the pool seemed almost jet-black against its virginal whiteness.

Lingering in the shallows, the White Sturgeon held very still. His was the accumulated wisdom of ages. Ancestors almost exactly like him had swum in antediluvian seas when huge, scaley monsters roamed the earth, and perhaps the White Sturgeon knew that, as long as he held still near the snow-covered bank, he would be hard to see. Or perhaps he merely found the snow, his own color matched at last, interesting.

Right after the snow stopped there was a spell of sub-zero weather that threw a sheathing of ice clear across the pool and froze the shallows to the very bottom. Only then did the White Sturgeon move out of them.

He did not move far because it was not necessary to move far, and anyway the great pike lingered in the center of the pool. Almost one third jaw, the pikes' mouths were edged with needle-sharp teeth that never let go and never failed to rip what they seized. Of the young sturgeon that lived until fall, perhaps two hundred and fifty in all, the pike had half before the winter was well set. The rest were too wary to be easy prey.

All winter long, living on the edge of the ice and finding all the food he needed in the soft mud floor of the pool, the White Sturgeon led a solitary existence. But it was not a lonely life because, as yet, it was not in him to be lonely. All he knew, and all he had to know, was that he must survive. Every effort was bent to that end.

In the spring, shortly after the ice broke up and moved sluggishly down the river, the White Sturgeon followed it. With him went three of his brothers and two sisters, and if more than that had survived he did not know about them or where they were. Nor did he care. In his life there was no room for or meaning to affection; he traveled with his brothers and sisters merely because, like him, they too were going down the river.

The journey was not at all hurried. The White Sturgeon, who by this time knew much more about the various arts of survival than he had known when he left the pool, passed the next winter in another, smaller pool, less than two miles from his birthplace. He chose the pool largely because it was the home of a vast number of fish smaller than he, and they offered an easy living to the pike, bass and other things that lived by eating fish. Grown fat and sluggish in the midst of super-abundance, these predators were not inclined to chase anything that cared to avoid them or to work at all for their living. All they had to do was lie still and sooner or later the living would come to them.

For his part, the White Sturgeon had no desire to hurt anything. His sole wish was to be left alone, so he could peacefully pursue his own path of destiny. He grubbed in the mud for his food and idled when he was not eating. But, because he had a prodigious appetite, he was eating most of the time. As a consequence, he continued to grow very rapidly.

Again and again, while he pursued his lazy journey down the river, the White Sturgeon saw the lake sturgeon swim past him as they headed upstream toward the spawning grounds. Swimming strongly, they came in huge schools. Spent from the spawning, they swam slowly past him on their way back to the lake.

Vaguely the White Sturgeon identified himself with these fish. Never did he have more than a passing wish to join them. He wanted only to continue his leisurely trip down the river, and time meant nothing at all.

Though the White Sturgeon did not realize it, everything was part of a mighty pattern and a vast scheme. Though there had never been a time when he was not in danger, the river had not been an unkind school. There he had learned how to avoid his enemies and how to become the powerful fish which he must be were he to live. Then the river gave him his last test.

He was near the mouth, only a few miles from the lake, when he suddenly found himself face to face with a monstrous pike. The pike in the pool of his birth were big, but they were dwarfed by this one. Out of the shadows he came, a long, sinewy thing with the heart of a tiger and the jaws of a pike. Even wolves' jaws are not more terrible.

The White Sturgeon did as he always did when danger threatened; he held very still. But this time it was futile because the pike had already seen him. Thus the thing which must never happen, did happen. The White Sturgeon came face to face with danger in its deadliest form. If he lived through this, then never again would he have to fear an enemy that swam in the water.

Suddenly the pike whirled, flipped a contemptuous tail, and drifted back into the shadows out of which he had come. He was not afraid; no pike is ever afraid of anything, but the White Sturgeon was nearly as large as he and even the pike never killed wantonly, or destroyed that which he could not eat. The White Sturgeon swam on. He had graduated with honors from the river's school, and he seemed to know it. For the first time since his birth, a mighty restlessness gripped him.

Not again did he linger in the pools, or stop to feed for a week or a month wherever he found a rich feeding bed. Urgings and commands within him that had been passive were suddenly active.

With all this, he remained a harmless fish. Never born to battle, he had no wish to fight and he did not abandon all his hard-won caution. If the pike had not hurt him, nothing that swam in the river or lake would hurt him; but the White Sturgeon retained a fear of those creatures not born of the water. Aliens, they would not abide by the creed of the water. While heeding a sudden and great wish to get out of the river and into the lake, the White Sturgeon stayed far from both river banks.

A ghost figure in the murky water, he shot out of the river's mouth and into the cold lake. For a while he sported like a dolphin, rising to the surface, showing his white back, and diving.

An Indian who was spearing fish from a canoe stared his astonishment. Trembling, he sheathed his spear and paddled back to his encampment. He had seen the White Sturgeon, the Ghost Fish, and that night a mighty storm knocked down a big pine near the Indian's camp. Two people were killed when it fell.

Knowing nothing of this, lying contentedly in thirty feet of water where he was aware of the storm only because his fine and deep senses made him aware of everything that occurred above, the White Sturgeon grubbed for food in the lake's bottom.

The next time his tribe left the lake to rush up the river, the White Sturgeon journeyed with them. He went because he must, because it was a call even stronger than hunger and he could not resist it. The strongest of sturgeon, he stayed in the fore-front of the spawning horde and still remained away from the banks. The few Indians who saw him were so astonished that they forgot to strike with their spears, and he never even came close to the prowling bears and other beasts that waxed so fat when the migrating sturgeon came back to spawn.

Guided by the most precise of instincts, the White Sturgeon went exactly to that spawning bed in the sedges where he was born, and fertilized the eggs that a female left there. Wan and spent, caring for nothing, once his main purpose in life had been realized, he turned and swam back into the lake. That was now his home.

Again and again the White Sturgeon went up the river with his kind. Only once, in all the trips he made, was he in real danger, and that time an Indian's spear scratched his side. The Indian, fishing with two companions, promptly fell into the river and drowned.

Thus the legend of the White Sturgeon grew. Born in a red man's fertile mind, it was handed from red man to white and distorted in the transfer. Now none could trace its origin and none knew exactly how it had begun. Lake men knew only of the White Sturgeon, and he had learned much of men. But he lived in the present, not the past.

Years had elapsed since Lake Michigan was shadowed only by canoes. Now there were the Mackinaw boats, the pound boats, the churning side-wheelers and the rowboats. Because it was his affair to know everything that went on in the lake, the White Sturgeon knew them all.

He knew also that it was good to rest in the lake's gentler places. Not in years had he rushed up the river with his spawning comrades. The fires of his youth had long since been quenched, and besides, he was now far too big to travel up any river. Perhaps the same quirk of nature that had granted him his pigment had given him his size. Other sturgeon were thought to be huge when they attained a weight of two hundred and fifty pounds. The White Sturgeon weighed almost a thousand pounds.

He was still a gentle creature, though the sudden angers of age were apt to seize him, and on the morning that Ramsay, Pieter and Hans were called to Three Points, the Sturgeon was feeding quietly in the tunnel of the first pound net they had set. He stopped feeding when he sensed an approaching boat.

It was a Mackinaw boat, used for setting gill nets, and it was shrouded in mist that sat like a fleecy blanket upon the lake. The White Sturgeon lay very still. He was not afraid but he had no wish to be disturbed, and if he remained very quiet, perhaps he would not be bothered. He was aware of something coming into the lake and of the boat's withdrawal into the shrouding mist.

The White Sturgeon decided to move, but when he tried to do so he found his way blocked. A gill net was stretched across the entrance to the pound net, effectively preventing anything outside from getting in or anything inside from getting out, and the White Sturgeon was trapped by it.

Gently he nosed against the gill net, seeking a way through. When none offered, he swam a little ways and tried again. A third, a fourth and a fifth time he sought escape. There was none, and the White Sturgeon's anger flared.

He flung himself against the gill net, felt it cling to his mighty body, and twisted about. A hundred yards to one side, in a weak place, the net ripped completely in half. The White Sturgeon threshed and twisted until he had reduced the entrapping folds to a mass of linen thread.

Segments of the ruined net clung to him as he swam away.

CHAPTER ELEVEN

FISHERMAN'S LUCK

The horse that had galloped from Three Points to Pieter's farm in order to bring news of Marta's misfortune was too spent to gallop back. Nor could he carry more than one man, even if he had not been spent. Ramsay, Pieter and Hans left horse and rider at the farm, while they started up the beach. For a short distance they stayed together. Then Ramsay, the youngest and best winded of the three, drew ahead.

A cold dread and a great fear gnawed at him as he alternately walked and trotted. Marta had become like a beloved sister to him, and the messenger carried no news except that she was injured. How or why, he had not said. Ramsay glanced back over his shoulder to see if his companions were keeping up with him, and discovered that they were lost in the mist. In any event the day would have been unpleasant. There was just the right weather combination to make it so—a hint of rain combined with warm air to drape the fog over everything. And there was no indication that anything would change. Somehow it seemed just the day to get bad news.

Ramsay lengthened out to trot again, and then increased his trot to a run. He was breathing hard, but far from exhausted, and with a little surprise he realized that he would not have been able to travel so far without halting, or so fast, when he first came to Wisconsin. A fisherman's life had toughened him immeasurably. Once more he slowed down and looked around to see if Pieter and Hans were in sight. They were not. He walked until he was rested, then trotted into Three Points.

As though there was something in the village that drove it back, the mist had not invaded there. It was on all sides so thick that the lake could not be seen and the trees were ghost shapes, half-concealed and half-disclosed. Most of Three Points was at work, but the few passers-by on the street glanced curiously at Ramsay as he swung past them. He saw the little black horse, tied to a hitching post in front of the general store.

He bounded up the wooden steps, pushed the door open and entered. Marta, the lower part of her left leg encased in a clean white bandage, was sitting on a chair. She turned astonished eyes on him. "Ramsay!"

"Are you all right?" he gasped.

"Why ... Of course, I'm all right!"

"You're not hurt?"

"A scratch!" She sniffed disdainfully. "Just a scratch! I stumbled when I stepped out of the cart. Ach! Such a clumsy one I was!"

The storekeeper's wife, obviously the one who had bandaged Marta's leg, smiled her reassurance. "It is not bad," she said.

"Oh!" Ramsay felt a moment's clumsiness because he could think of nothing to say, and again he exclaimed, "Oh!"

Panting hard, deep concern written on their faces, Hans and Pieter came into the store. Marta's surprised eyes opened still wider. "I thought you boys were fishing!"

"We—we had to come in for some more twine," Ramsay said somewhat lamely.

"Three of you?"

"Yaah," Hans, never slow to understand, smiled with affected laziness. "You know us men, Marta. There wouldn't one of us stay there and work while another was loafing in Three Points."

"That's right." Slow Pieter finally understood that there was more here than met the eye. "How'd you hurt yourself, Marta?"

The wondering gaze of the storekeeper and his wife were upon them now. Still puzzled, Marta glanced covertly at the three men. Ramsay looked at the storekeeper's wife.

"You should have sent somebody to tell us she was hurt."

"But," the storekeeper's wife was completely bewildered, "she is not hurt."

"What's the matter?" Marta seemed worried now.

"Nothing," Hans answered blandly. "Nothing at all. We just decided to have a holiday in Three Points."

"Go long!" Marta scoffed. "Men! They're bigger babies than babies are!"

"Be sure to bring us some twine," Hans said.

"Oh, sure. That I will do."

"Good."

All three men were smiling easily. But as soon as they left the store and were out of Marta's sight, the smiles faded and their faces became grim and intent.

"Who was the man who told us she was hurt?" Ramsay asked.

Pieter shook his head, and Hans said, "I never saw him before and I don't expect to see him again. Probably he was riding into Milwaukee anyway, and somebody gave him a dollar to report an accident."

Ramsay nodded. Hans, as usual, was logical and there could be only one answer. Somebody was indeed out to capture the fishing on Lake Michigan. They had started by destroying Baptiste's nets and now they were moving against Ramsay and his friends. But they knew well the prowess of the three and had no wish to strike while they were present. Marta's reported accident had been only a ruse to draw them away.

Ramsay started toward the sand beach, but Hans laid a restraining hand on his shoulder. "Wait!"

"We'd better get back and look to our nets."

"There is time, and we'd better not go blindly."

"What are we going to do?"

Hans said grimly, "Find the constable and ask him to accompany us. Then, if there is trouble, and I expect it, we will have the law with us rather than against us."

"Suppose the constable doesn't care to come along?"

"He'll come," Hans promised.

They strolled down the street, stopping in various places, until they found Jake Hillis, the constable Devil Chad had put in office, in the Lake House. The woman who had given Ramsay the steak and then made him wash dishes to pay for it, looked up and smiled. "Hello."

"Hi!" Ramsay grinned.

"You didn't run, after all."

"Nope. I didn't."

The constable, standing at the bar, turned around to face the three. He hooked both thumbs in his belt, letting his fingers dangle. His right hand, Ramsay could not help seeing, was not too far from the pistol that swung from his belt. There was no readable expression on his face, but the woman, who knew him well, went hastily into another room.

Flanked by Ramsay and Pieter, Hans walked directly up to the constable.

"We have something," he said softly, "that demands your attention."

"What is it?"

"It has to do with nets and a raid upon them."

"I got no authority over what happens on Lake Michigan."

"Nevertheless, we need a good, honest man of the law with us. And we will pay you well enough."

Jake Hillis shook his head. "I can't go off on any wild goose chases. My duty is to protect this town."

Hans' voice softened even more. "I am asking you again to come with us."

The constable's right thumb slipped from his belt and his hand dropped to the butt of the revolver. His fingers curled around it. As though by accident, Pieter stumbled forward. Strong enough to stop a bull in its tracks, Pieter wrapped his own steel fingers around the constable's right wrist, and when they disengaged the pistol was in Pieter's hand.

"Excuse me!" he said contritely. "I am so clumsy!"

"Well?" Hans inquired.

Jake Hillis looked from one to the other. He was like a drum which almost always must sound the cadence someone else beats. Strength was the only force he recognized, and now he saw himself surrounded by strong, determined men. For a moment he struggled with himself. Then "I'll go," he said.

Hans responded graciously, "Thank you. We knew that you would come as soon as you understood the reason in it."

"Here's your pistol." Pieter extended the weapon.

"I got to warn you," the constable pronounced, "that I am going to hold you responsible for anything that happens here while I am away. And I better tell you that I won't put up with any law-breaking."

"Good!" Hans said. "You are a conscientious man!"

The mist dipped and twisted about them as they started down the sand beach toward Pieter's farm. Ramsay tried to find answers to the many questions in his mind. Certainly somebody had lured them away from their fishing gear. Who had done so? Was Devil Chad involved? If so, why did Jake Hillis accompany them at all? Certainly the servant would not willingly provoke a fight with the master. If Devil Chad was the leader of the pirates, did he trust his minion so little that he had told him nothing?

Ramsay shrugged: they would have to wait and find out.

Reaching the farm, Pieter entered the house to get the shotgun and a pair of exquisitely carved pistols which Ramsay had never seen before. Dueling pistols, they looked like, and Ramsay glanced curiously at Pieter. The man was anything except stolid, yet he never spoke of his past and of what had really brought him across the Atlantic Ocean to this wild inland sea. Ramsay dismissed the thought. In this country it was often just as well to forget a man's past or that he had ever had a past.

Jake Hillis looked narrowly as Pieter handed Hans a pistol, kept one for himself and gave the shotgun to Ramsay. "I don't hold with shooting scrapes!" he said. "And I don't want any part of 'em!"

"There'll be none," Hans assured him, "unless we are shot at first."

They launched a pound boat, and Hans took the rower's seat. Jake Hillis sat beside Pieter and Ramsay crouched to one side. A shiver ran through him. The mist seemed to be settling in even more thickly; they had scarcely left the shore when they were unable to see it. From the top of the house, the bedraggled Captain Klaus squawked his protest at such weather.

Hans rowed swiftly but there was no trace of hesitation in his manner, and Ramsay marveled. The mist was heavy enough to cut visibility to almost nothing, but Hans steered as certainly as he would have on the sunniest of days. He seemed to know the lake so intimately that, no matter what happened, he could still find his way. They reached the first pound net, rowed around it. Ramsay sighed with relief.

If pirates had come to raid, they had not yet touched this net. Ramsay shifted his position, and Jake Hillis stirred uneasily. Then, almost beside the boat, the water rippled and the White Sturgeon surfaced for a moment. Nearly the color of the mist, he lay quietly on top of the water, then dived.

Hans' low laughter rippled. "We have a friend!" he said.

They were near the second pound net now, and Ramsay gripped his shotgun fiercely. He could see nothing, but something seemed to be present. It was a half-sensed threat, like an unseen tiger crouching in the darkness beside a campfire. They saw the spiles of the second pound net rising like a ghost's fingers. Slowly Hans started rowing around it.

Then Ramsay glanced behind him and snapped the shotgun to his shoulder. From shorewards another mist-wreathed craft appeared. It was a Mackinaw boat, like the *Spray*, and the men on her were only half seen in the heavy overcast. Ramsay breathed a warning, "Watch it!"

Hans let the boat drift and took the pistol in his hand. Almost carelessly, as though there was no hurry about anything at all, Pieter did likewise. Jake Hillis drew his breath sharply. The two boats came closer together, and Ramsay recognized Joe Mannis. There were also three nondescript loafers of the riff-raff type who are always found on any frontier and who will do anything for money. But Ramsay centered his gaze on the fifth man in the Mackinaw boat.

There could be no mistaking him, even in the mist. It was Devil Chad.

The other boat came nearer and was much easier to see. Ramsay felt a cold chill seize him. All the men in the boat were armed with shotguns, and they could sweep the pound boat from one end to the other if there was to be a fight. Ramsay glanced at Jake Hillis. The constable was sitting quietly, tense and strained, but he did not seem to be afraid.

Devil Chad's bellow blasted, "What are you doin' here?"

Ramsay heard Hans' low laugh and his quiet, "The man is most uncivil."

"Don't get smart with me!" Devil Chad threatened. "You come to rob our net, didn't you?"

Hans, surprised, made a momentary slip. "Your net?"

"Yes, our net! You come to rob it like you robbed all the rest!" Chad's expressionless eyes pierced Jake Hillis like daggers. "What are you doin' here?"

Hans answered calmly. "He is here as our guest, and at our invitation. Now let us hear some more about 'your' net."

"You know what I mean! Touch it an' we start shootin'!"

"But we haven't touched anything," Hans said smilingly. He turned to Jake Hillis. "Have we?"

Jake Hillis, too dull-witted for quick evasion, said, "No, you haven't."

Cold rage mounted within Ramsay. He swung his shotgun so that the muzzle centered squarely on Devil Chad. If it came to a gun battle, he decided grimly, his arch-enemy would at least be shot at.

Hans, unruffled, took command. "Where is your net? Show us."

"Right here."

Ramsay heard the mockery in Hans' voice. "And I suppose that it is a gill net?"

"How'd you know that?" Devil Chad challenged.

"I gazed into my crystal ball," Hans said smoothly, "and I discovered that, when one fisherman wishes to eliminate a competitor, he can always stretch a gill net across the tunnel of a pound net. There is certain to be a battle, and whoever survives controls the fishing."

Ramsay began to understand. Fishing on Lake Michigan was governed by no enforceable law but only by the ethics of the fishermen themselves. Most of them were ethical; when one found a good fishing ground, others usually respected his rights. But there was no law that said they had to respect them. Should one fisherman care to trespass on the rights of another, he could always find some way to provoke a quarrel. Then, regardless of anything else that happened, he could say that he was only trying to protect his property or claim in some other way that his was a just quarrel. Few people would be able to prove to the contrary.

Then a blue-and-white buoy, a marker used on a gill net, floated into sight. Hans saw it, too, and again his voice was mocking. "Is that the net you mean?"

There were subdued voices on the Mackinaw boat. Joe Mannis put his shotgun down and stepped to the bow of the boat with a gaff hook in his hand. He lay prone, stabbed with the gaff, and hooked the buoy. Foot by foot he reeled in thirty yards of tattered gill net. Hans' scornful laughter rolled like a barrel through the mist and bounded back in echoes. Ramsay, highly amused, echoed Hans.

"Find your other buoy!" Hans called. "Pull it in, take it home, and repair your gill net! But do not again set it on our fishing grounds!"

The Mackinaw boat floated into the mist. Ramsay saw the baffled rage on Devil Chad's face. But mostly he was aware of the contempt of Hans for Devil Chad.

"Here!" Hans called. "You're missing a man!" He turned to Jake Hillis. The constable glowered back, like a stupid horse.

"Want to swim over and join your little friends?" Hans invited.

"No."

"Well, we brought you out from the sand. We'll take you back to the sand."

Hans' shoulders were shaking with silent mirth as he bent his back to the pound boat's oars. He steered in to the pier they had built, and expertly nosed the boat in to its landing. A mist-draped wraith, Marta, awaited them. "What happened?" she queried anxiously.

"Nothing," Pieter assured her.

"A great deal," Hans corrected. "They caught the White Sturgeon, for no other fish in the lake could have wrecked a net so completely. I told you we have a friend."

He took a pouch from his pocket, counted five silver dollars from it, and dropped them into Jake Hillis' hand. Captain Klaus flew down from the house top to alight on Hans' shoulder. "*Quark!*" he squawked.

As though he understood perfectly, Hans said, "That is right, my little one." And to Jake Hillis he said, "If you see them, tell them not to come again."

Deliberately turning his back on the constable, Hans stared out over the lake. Then Jake Hillis was gone, and somehow it was as though he had never even been with them. Ramsay waited expectantly. Hans turned away from his intent study of the lake, and he was frowning as though there was some complicated problem which he must solve. Yet when he spoke, his voice betrayed nothing abnormal and there was no sign that he might have been under the least strain. "Perhaps it would be well not to fish again today. That is a shame, for the season draws to a close and we cannot fish much longer, anyway. Still, we have done all that it is necessary to do, and next year we will be well-situated. We will have gear and tackle. I go to work on the boat."

Ramsay asked, "Do you think they will come again?"

Hans answered deliberately, "I do not think so, but no man may say for certain. They are not without determined and intelligent leadership. If he does come again, he will come hard and directly at us. He will not bother with the nets. There is no need to keep a patrol on the lake tonight."

Without another word Hans turned on his heel and strode off to where the *Spray II* was supported on its blocks. Ramsay went into the barn, shouldered a hundred-pound sack of cornmeal, and carried it to the pond in which he had imprisoned almost countless sturgeon. With both hands he cast the ground corn into the pool, and returned for another sack, and another. Then he stood with the last empty sack limp in his hands, idly watching the pond.

It had been an exciting summer, the most adventurous and most satisfying he could remember, but it must soon end.

Already there was a hint of frost in the air, and frost meant that the whitefish would soon spawn. Nothing could persuade Hans to fish in the spawning season, when every fish caught meant the loss of perhaps ten that might be. Even if Hans would have fished, autumn meant storms when none but a fool would venture onto the lake in a small boat.

Ramsay turned slowly away from the pond. He wandered over to where Hans was working on the *Spray II*. It was to be a Mackinaw boat, somewhat like a canoe, and it was to be used for setting gill nets. These, Ramsay understood, could be set almost as soon as the ice went out.

Handy with almost any sort of tool, Hans himself had fashioned a wood vise that turned on a wooden gear. He had a section of cedar stump clamped in the vise, and with a rasp and a fine-toothed saw he was painstakingly fashioning a rib for the *Spray II*. Unhurried, a true artist, he shaped one side of the rib to the other. When he had finished, it was a perfect thing, so evenly balanced that a feather's weight on either side might have unbalanced it. Ramsay wandered away, satisfied. The *Spray II* was to be no ordinary vessel. There would not be another Mackinaw boat on Lake Michigan to match it.

Restlessly Ramsay worked on the seine until Marta called them. He ate, went to bed, and dropped into his usual instant deep slumber.

At first he was vaguely irritated because noises in the night disturbed him. Then he identified those sounds as the crying of an alarmed sea gull. Captain Klaus, on top of the roof, was vehemently protesting something. Ramsay became aware of a strange, unreal sunrise reflecting through his bedroom window.

Fully awake, he rushed to the window, and saw that, down on the beach, all their boats were burning fiercely.

CHAPTER TWELVE

THE POND

Captain Klaus made a swooping flight that carried him out toward the burning boats. Frightened by a puff of smoke, he flew back to the top of the house and continued to call querulously.

For a moment Ramsay stood still, petrified by the spectacle. Then his shout alarmed the house. "Hans! Pieter!"

By the light that flickered through his window he sprang for his clothing and hastily pulled his trousers on. Letting the tails and front hang out, he donned his shirt and put shoes on his bare feet. He was aware of muffled cries echoing from the rest of the house, and a lighted candle flared in the hall.

He rushed out to meet Hans coming from his bedroom, and a second later Pieter's door flew open. Only half-awake and less than half-dressed, the latter blinked like a sleepy dog in the candle's little light.

Marta peered uneasily over his shoulder. "What is it?"

"The boats are burning!" Ramsay gasped.

With a mighty, outraged lion's roar, Pieter came fully awake and sprang toward the stairs. For one brief second Ramsay was aware of Marta's face, dead-white, then he leaped to follow Pieter. Holding the candle aloft, Hans followed. Again the Dutch fisherman seemed to take complete command of the situation. There was anger in his voice but no trace of panic when he warned the other two, "Slowly! Go slowly!"

His hand on the kitchen door, Pieter halted. Ramsay paused uncertainly behind him, and Hans blew the candle out. The Dutch fisherman had weathered so many savage storms that he seemed to know exactly what to do, no matter what the crisis. Ramsay watched and approved. He must learn to be more like Hans and to rule the emergencies that arose rather than let them rule him.

Hans spoke again, "Let us not go like sheep to the slaughter. If they came again, they are probably armed and they may shoot. Pieter, get the guns."

Pieter shuffled off to the dark kitchen and came back. Ramsay felt the familiar shotgun being pressed into his hands, and he knew that Hans and Pieter each had a pistol. Because that seemed the thing to do, Ramsay waited until Hans acted. The Dutch fisherman spoke again, and his voice remained unruffled. "We cannot tell who or what is out there. Until we discover exactly, keep out of the light cast by the burning boats. Do not use your guns unless they shoot first. Then shoot to kill. Come on."

Silent as a shadow, Hans slipped into the blackness that reigned at the back of the house. Pieter followed, while Ramsay brought up the rear. He shivered, but only part of his chill was caused by the cold night. This afternoon on the pound boat he had felt only tense excitement. But then Hans and Pieter had backed him and their presence had been a very real thing. Now, in the night, he was almost completely unaware of them. It was as though he stood completely alone.

Ramsay felt his way along the rear wall of the house to the corner, and there the darkness was broken by the glare from the burning boats. Ramsay crept up beside Hans and peered around the corner.

The mist was gone, and a sharp breeze had sprung up in its wake. Every night, when the fishing was done, or any time at all when they weren't being used, the pound boats were pulled far up on the shore. Casting a circle of light over the water, the burning boats illuminated the rising waves whose whitecaps broke and fell. A fierce storm was in the making.

Ramsay's fear gave way to terrible anger. The wind from the lake would have fanned the flames anyway, but obviously, before they had been set on fire, the two pound boats had been coated with tar, pitch, or something else that would burn hard and assure their complete destruction. They were already charred beyond the faintest hope of salvation. Ramsay gritted his teeth.

Hans left the house and swung back, away from the lake, on a course that would keep him in the shadows. Ramsay followed, and he was aware of Pieter following him. There was not the least sign of the raiders or of the boat they might have come in. Ramsay hesitated. Perhaps they had done their work and fled, or perhaps they were lurking in ambush near the burning boats. Five shotguns could be ready to cut down whoever came.

Then Ramsay set all his doubts at rest. He knew what he must do.

There could no longer be any question but that this was Devil Chad's work. He controlled everything around Three Points that made any money. He was out to gain control of the fishing, too, and he was not a man who would leave any job half-done. Failing to provoke a fight because the White Sturgeon had ruined his gill net, he had taken the direct approach. Beyond any doubt he would be able to produce any number of witnesses who would swear that Hans, Ramsay and Pieter were the aggressors. Ramsay knew what he was going to do about this.

"Take the shotgun," he whispered, and pressed the weapon upon Pieter.

"But ..."

"Take it," Ramsay repeated.

Leaving the shotgun with the bewildered Pieter, he dropped to the ground and wormed farther away from the circle of light. Into the shadows he went, then on toward the lake. Now he did not know where Hans and Pieter were or what they were doing, but he was positive that they would take any action necessary when the time came. He no longer felt alone.

This was a thing that could never be settled with guns but must be slugged out toe to toe and man to man. The fishing was worthwhile, and any man who would get and keep anything worthwhile had to be ready to fight for it. If Devil Chad had already fled, tomorrow they must go into Three Points and seek him out.

Ramsay halted, peering around. He could see nothing clearly. The flames had died down and there was only dimness, filled with varying shadows that were most difficult to identify. But what was that down at the edge of the lake?

It seemed to rise and fall with the rising and falling waves. Most of the shadows were there one second and flitted away the next, but this did not flit away, and after another thirty seconds Ramsay was fairly sure that it was a Mackinaw boat, anchored out in the lake. Its crew had waded ashore from it and, when and if they ran, they would wade back to it.

Ramsay began a slow, steady crawl toward the anchored craft. The burning pound boats flared brightly, seeming to ring him with a halo of light. He shrank back, certain he could be seen, then as the glare subsided, crawled forward again. If he could see no one in the darkness, neither could anyone see him.

He was within thirty yards of the lake now, and he no longer gave a thought to Hans and Pieter. He was sure only that they would be present when they were needed and that his way was the right one. There could be no compromise with destruction and no lingering aftermath of this outrage. Whatever was to be settled had to be settled completely, and tonight.

Ramsay was certain now that the thing he saw was an anchored Mackinaw boat. It remained in the same place, rising and falling with the waves, and no nebulous shadow did that. Intent on the boat, he was not aware of the man until he heard his voice, "Gus, you fool! I said be quiet!"

Ramsay held very still, and a rising exultation flooded him. He had heard that voice before, and there was only one just like it. He had heard it first when he stood on the *Holter*—that seemed years ago. He knew that he lay within feet of Devil Chad, who was indeed waiting in ambush with his men.

The angry voice repeated, "Be quiet! They'll come!"

Ramsay rose and rushed forward, flinging himself into this combat with all the fierce joy of a newly awakened warrior. He had given a full summer, an important part of his life, to building up a career which he greatly loved. Now he stood ready to defend it with his muscles, his heart and, if need be, his life.

He saw Devil Chad rise uncertainly to meet him, not knowing whether he was friend or foe. He aimed a mighty kick at the shotgun in the other's hands, and he knew that he had knocked it completely out of his enemy's grasp. He felt a fresh burst of wind on his cheek and, strangely, knew all about the storm that was brewing on the great lake. He closed with his enemy.

Devil Chad and his men had come to destroy and, if necessary, to kill. But they had counted on Ramsay, Pieter and Hans, charging angrily up the sand beach. Outlined against the burning boats, they would be at a tremendous disadvantage. A hail of lead from five shotguns could cut them down in almost no time. They had their choice between surrendering or dying for what they believed in.

It had never occurred to Devil Chad or his men that an enemy would dare crawl into their very midst. The darkness that had befriended them now became their enemy. Nobody dared shoot because nobody could possibly be certain whether he were shooting at friend or foe. Ramsay edged up to Devil Chad and swung a tremendous upper-cut to the other's jaw.

He missed, felt his knuckles graze his enemy's cheek, and stepped back for a new try. Only vaguely was he aware of muffled exclamations that became shouts and then grunts. He knew that Pieter and Hans had closed in. Then it was as though he and Devil Chad were alone.

This was something that had to be. The seed that made the task necessary had been planted long ago, on the *Holter*. It had taken deep root during the fight in the tannery. Since that time Ramsay had met every challenge the lake had flung at him. Now he would have to prove himself capable of meeting the challenges men flung at him. Then, and only then, could he survive.

Ramsay's lips framed a grin. He had taken the risk, and he had won. For one brief second somebody might have shot him down, then the opportunity was forever gone. Now nobody dared shoot. He found a firm footing on the lake sand.

Ramsay dodged a terrific blow that would have knocked him flat had it connected, and went back in with his arms swinging. He sunk a left and a right to his adversary's midriff and heard Devil Chad's breath whistle out of his clenched lips. He drew back to strike again.

Like the bull he was, Devil Chad charged recklessly. He took Ramsay's stinging blows without flinching, and the boy had to give ground. But it was not lost ground, and for one brief, glorious second Ramsay stood and traded blows. His head rocked, but he took what the other had to offer and returned it in full measure. Then he learned his mistake.

A pair of gigantic arms were flung about his middle. They tightened like a vise, bending him backward and seeming to compress him into a space not half-big enough. His spine was ready to crack, and lights danced in his head. He gasped for air.

The many lessons he had been taught by Hans Van Doorst came to his rescue. Four months ago, and perhaps even one month ago, the fight would have been ended by that terrific bear hug. But now Ramsay remembered in time that he was not fighting a man alone but a man who was part beast. And it was never wise to lose one's head. A man must always adapt himself and fight like a beast if he fought with one.

Summoning all his remaining strength, Ramsay drew back his right foot and sent his heavy shoe smashing into Devil Chad's shin. The fellow relaxed his hold and staggered back into the darkness.

Ramsay stumbled away from him. Devil Chad was a bull, he remembered, and he did not know about matadors. The next time he rushed, the boy stepped aside and let his opponent's momentum carry him past. Ramsay's strength and breath came back.

He became cool, able to reason coolly. Devil Chad outweighed him by fifty pounds, so he must not close again. If he did not, and there were no accidents, he, Ramsay, would win this fight. For the first time in his life Devil Chad was fighting his equal.

Ramsay felt strength swell within him. It was the strength of the lake, and it had flowed into his body through the numberless sturgeon he had carried to the pond and from the many times he had helped bring in the seine and from the many fish he had scooped from the raised pound nets. He was no longer a boy but a man.

The burning pound boats were falling into embers now, and as the light they cast receded the blackness of the night became more intense. Wind keened in from the lake, and the waves assaulting the sand beach made themselves heard.

Ramsay waded in, his fists flying. In the darkness he was aware of Devil Chad coming to meet him, but his deception of his opponent was complete. From the first, he had had no intention of meeting him squarely.

He stepped aside, lashing out with both fists as he did so, and felt both of them collide soddenly with Devil Chad's chin. The latter bellowed, swung his head and hooked viciously. But he hooked falsely, for Ramsay was not there. His lithe body, dodging and twisting, now here and now there, became like the cape that lures the bull to its doom. Devil Chad swung and kicked, and often he struck his target. But he did not strike hard enough to bring Ramsay down, and he could not again get a grip with his giant arms, although he tried desperately.

Roaring wildly, he charged. But it was a blind, mad attack, directed almost completely by rage and desperation.

Ramsay licked his upper lip, vaguely aware of the fact that he was tasting his own blood but not caring. He felt no pain, and it was oddly as though he sat on some high pinnacle from which he could watch himself and direct himself. Both his fists lashed squarely into Devil Chad's face, driven by all the strength in his hard, young body.

Devil Chad paused, as though bewildered, and Ramsay knew that he was stunned. Not stopping, throwing some of his caution to the wind, he followed up his advantage. His fists worked like cracking whips as he struck again and again. Devil Chad spun around, took two halting steps, and sank to one knee.

He remained there like some carved statue, and again Ramsay licked away the blood that flowed down his face. Now, if he did the correct thing, he would go in and end it with kicking feet. He would beat Devil Chad as mercilessly as he had been beaten. But he did not.

He waited, cool and poised, while the other bowed before him. Only when Devil Chad lurched to his feet and struck out drunkenly did Ramsay go in again, and he went in with his fists. He beat a continuous, almost unopposed tatto on his enemy's chin. The second time Devil Chad collapsed he measured his full length on the sand, and he did not move again.

Ramsay stood watching intently for several moments. He wanted to make certain that he had met his enemy fairly and defeated him fairly. How long he had been fighting he did not know. It seemed like a few seconds, but it must have been much longer. He only knew that he had come out of the battle stronger than he was when he went into it. He called, "Hans?"

"Here," the Dutch fisherman answered.

His voice was strained, but even now there was nothing of desperation in it. Rather, it was a joyous voice. Ramsay turned toward it and saw scuffling men. He approached them and reached out with groping hands until he touched another man. It was neither Hans nor Pieter, and as soon as he was sure of that he swung.

He felt a strong disappointment, for the heat of battle flared strong within him and, instead of fighting back, the man merely collapsed on the sand. Obviously he had already been manhandled by Hans and had little strength left. Ramsay looked strangely at him, as though there was something that should not be. Then he became aware of the fact that dawn had come and he could see. He turned to help Hans or Pieter, whichever needed it the most, and he turned just in time to see Hans hit Joe Mannis so hard that the body-watcher flew into the air, described a little backward whirl, and fell on the sand.

Hans stood, shaggy and huge, breathing hard, but unbeaten and unbeatable. Moving over beside him, Ramsay felt that at last he was worthy to stand there. Both watched while Pieter teased the single remaining man, one of the hired ruffians who had helped set the gill net, then slapped him resoundingly on both cheeks. As though he were unworthy of further notice, Pieter whirled on his heel and left his foe. The man went weaving up the beach into the lightening morning.

Hans grinned wryly at Ramsay. "Your face, it looks like a horse stepped on it."

"You've got a couple of mosquito bites yourself."

"Yaah." Hans grinned again.

Ramsay said, "They got our boats."

Hans said, "They got our nets, too. Joe Mannis, he told me that when we fought. They would get us, he said."

"They didn't."

"No, they didn't."

They turned at a sudden wooden scraping out on the lake, and saw the Mackinaw boat under way. Beaten and bruised, Devil Chad crouched at the oars. Hurriedly he sent the boat farther out, toward the open lake. They watched as though this were some foreign sight of no interest whatever.

Hans walked over to prod Joe Mannis with the toe of his shoe. "Get up," he said.

Joe Mannis stirred and groaned. He opened his eyes, blinked stupidly and raised himself on one hand. There was a deceptive gentleness in Hans' words and tone, but Joe Mannis was not deceived. He knew that Hans meant it when he said, "Come down the beach once more after this storm. You will find something to interest only you. Then never let me see you again. If I do, I will drown you in the lake."

Hans looked out on the lake, into the gathering storm and at the receding Mackinaw boat. High waves were already clawing at it, and Devil Chad was not yet out of the bay. Hans said, "He is not a fisherman. He is not even a sailor. I myself would think twice about taking the *Spray* out now."

Near the boat something white, something not born of the rolling whitecaps, appeared for a second and disappeared. Ramsay smiled softly. He knew that he had again seen the White Sturgeon. He also knew what Joe Mannis would find in the morning. Devil Chad.

The three partners walked back down the sand to the embers of the pound boats. They stood near them, warming themselves in the last of the fire. Ramsay prodded the sand with his toe.

They were right back where they had started. A whole summer's hard work had gone to satisfy the greed and lust of one man. What they had left was the seine, the row boat, the forming skeleton of the *Spray II* and the pier. Ramsay set his jaw. They could do it again. They had done it once.

He looked toward the Mackinaw boat, and discovered that it had gone out of the bay into the open lake. But his eyes were attracted by something else on the horizon.

A moment later he identified it as a plume of smoke. Five minutes afterward, storm-lashed but defiant, the *Jackson* nosed out of the lake into the sheltered bay. Manned by able seamen, sure of herself, the *Jackson* came up to her accustomed place at the pier. Ramsay, Hans and Pieter caught her mooring ropes.

Resplendent in his uniform, little Captain Williamson came down his rope ladder and strutted on the pier. "A blow," he said, as though a storm on Lake Michigan meant nothing to him. "We'll tie up here until it's over, then go back to Chicago. Have you got any fish?"

"Some," Ramsay admitted.

He thought of the ten barrels of whitefish that were ready for shipment, and he watched Captain Williamson's face fall. The little captain emitted a long sigh. "Some, eh? I was hoping for better news. Chicago's growing like a weed in the sun, and it's hungry. Most of the fishermen made their last shipments ten days ago. The markets are almost empty, and even sturgeon's bringing five cents a pound."

For one brief second the storm clouds parted and the sun shone through. Then the sky was again overcast and the storm leaped furiously. Ramsay turned his shining face toward Hans and Pieter. The tons of sturgeon in the pond ... At five cents a pound there would be more than enough money to replace everything and to buy the finest planking for the *Spray II*.

Ramsay said, "Save plenty of room on the *Jackson*. We'll need it."

On top of the ridge-pole, Captain Klaus fluttered his long wings and curved his sinuous neck. As though he approved thoroughly he called, "*Quark!*"

9 789361 471216